Nightmare Mansion

Nightmare Mansion

Matthew Petchinsky

Nightmare Mansion: The Labyrinth of Screams
By: Matthew Petchinsky

Prologue: The Aftermath of Failure

The crimson hue of the blood moon cast an eerie glow over the small town of Ravenswood, once a quiet, unassuming place nestled between rolling hills and dense forests. Now, it was nothing but a memory—a whisper of a town, swallowed by forces beyond mortal comprehension. What had once been streets lined with homes and businesses had become the domain of unspeakable horrors, each corner haunted by the echoes of the screams that filled the air on the night of the military's last stand.

It had begun as a military intervention—an organized, strategic assault on what the media dubbed *Nightmare Mansion*, a centuries-old structure at the heart of the town. For years, rumors had swirled about the mansion, its dark history of death and disappearances, but it wasn't until the blood moon's rise that everything changed. The air grew heavy, the sky darkened, and the mansion became a beacon of malevolent power, pulling the surrounding area into its expanding grasp. The military, summoned to contain what was thought to be a localized threat, had no idea what awaited them.

Armed to the teeth, they had entered Ravenswood under the assumption that they were dealing with a cult, or perhaps an insurgent force. Soldiers, tanks, and helicopters descended on the town, ready to quash whatever evil lurked in the shadows. But the horrors that greeted them were far beyond anything their training had prepared them for.

What had been designed as a tactical operation quickly spiraled into chaos. The first sign that something was terribly wrong came when the communication lines went dead—radios crackled and fell silent, cutting off their only connection to the outside world. Then came the screams. Echoing through the streets, unnatural, guttural sounds filled the air, and the soldiers found themselves face-to-face with monstrosities that defied logic. Creatures born from nightmares emerged from the fog, their forms ever-shifting, twisted beyond recognition.

Reports from survivors—those few unlucky enough to escape—painted a picture of unimaginable terror. Men were torn apart by unseen forces, shadows came alive, and the mansion itself seemed to warp reality, twisting space and time to trap its victims. Some soldiers swore they saw visions of their loved ones, their families calling out to them from within the mansion's walls, luring them to their deaths. Others found themselves endlessly running through hallways that stretched into infinity, only to be caught by something lurking just beyond their line of sight.

In the days that followed, the town of Ravenswood vanished from the map, consumed by an ever-expanding curse that swallowed the surrounding caverns and forest. The Nightmare Mansion, now an eldritch entity unto itself, had grown, its malignant presence spreading like a cancer. The once beautiful woods had become twisted, gnarled landscapes where reality bent and fractured, leaving those who ventured too close either dead or hopelessly insane. The caverns beneath the town, long rumored to connect to the mansion's ancient catacombs, opened up, revealing new depths teeming with otherworldly abominations.

The international community was quick to react, though not with the expected aid and relief efforts. Instead, there was outrage, confusion, and fear. How could a town be consumed so completely, its people eradicated without explanation? Speculation ran rampant. Was this a chemical attack? A biological weapon gone wrong? Or something more nefarious, something that even the world's governments couldn't—or wouldn't—explain?

Amidst the outrage, conspiracy theories flourished. Some believed that the military had provoked the horrors within the mansion, that their presence had triggered something ancient and unholy. Others whispered of government experiments gone awry, of dark rituals performed in secret by those in power. Official statements remained elusive, offering no clear answers, and so the world watched in horror as Ravenswood became a ghost story, a warning of what could happen when humanity delves too deeply into the unknown.

Yet, despite the outcry, no one dared approach the site again. Satellite images showed only a dense fog hanging over the area, obscuring the mansion and the surrounding terrain from view. Rescue missions were proposed, but quickly abandoned. Too many lives had already been lost, and those who remained knew better than to tempt fate a second time.

The Nightmare Mansion had become more than just a cursed house—it had become a living, breathing entity, growing with every soul it claimed. The town of Ravenswood was gone, and the forest and caverns had been consumed, but it was only a matter of time before the mansion's hunger would spread further, reaching into neighboring towns, cities, and perhaps, one day, the world beyond.

As the prologue to the disaster ended, so too did any hope of re-demption. The aftermath of failure was complete. All that remained was silence, and the distant, unholy howls carried on the wind—a haunting reminder of the forces that now ruled Ravenswood. The world, it seemed, had lost one of its battles against the supernatural. The question remained: how many more would follow?

Chapter 1: Gathering the Experts

The sterile glow of fluorescent lights flickered overhead as the members of the international task force filed into the conference room. It was a hastily organized meeting, one born out of desperation after the military's disastrous failure. The air buzzed with tension, palpable to anyone who entered the room, and seated around the long, oak table were men and women who, until this day, had never crossed paths—leaders of science, mysticism, and everything in between.

At the head of the table sat General Richard Donovan, a grizzled veteran whose scarred face spoke of countless battles, though none as terrifying as the one looming ahead. To his left was Dr. Eleanor Blackwood, a physicist who specialized in atomic theory, her sharp mind concealed behind an icy demeanor. Across from her sat Professor Marcus Brandt, an expert in metaphysics with an impressive knowledge of the paranormal, his weathered hands tapping nervously on the table. Next to him was Imogen Reed, a high-ranking practitioner of Wicca, her long silver hair falling loosely over a deep emerald cloak, and to her right, the dark-eyed occultist, Sergei Volkov, known in underground circles for his dangerous knowledge of forbidden magicks.

As the last members took their seats, Donovan cleared his throat. "Thank you all for coming on such short notice," he began, his gravelly voice resonating in the hushed room. "I don't have to tell you why we're here. Ravenswood is gone. The Nightmare Mansion is growing. The military... failed."

A silence fell over the room as Donovan allowed the weight of his words to sink in. Sergei was the first to speak, his accent thick but clear. "You cannot fight the supernatural with guns and bombs, General. This is no ordinary threat. The forces at play here are ancient, far older than any government or military."

"Which is why we're here," Donovan replied, his patience visibly wearing thin. "We know the threat isn't physical. That's why we've brought together a team that covers every angle—metaphysics, mythology, magick, and yes, science. Whatever this mansion is, it's drawing power from somewhere, and if we don't figure out how to stop it, it's going to consume more than just Ravenswood."

Imogen nodded, her voice soft yet firm. "The Wiccan community has long felt the disturbance coming from that place. I sensed it years ago, but none of us could predict the scale. It's tied to the lunar cycles—the blood moon, specifically. If it continues to draw power from the celestial events, it will be nearly impossible to contain."

Eleanor leaned forward, her expression skeptical. "You're talking about *magick* as if it's a quantifiable force. I deal in atoms, in measurable energy. I fail to see how we're supposed to approach this scientifically."

Brandt, who had remained silent until now, smiled thinly. "Dr. Blackwood, you may find that science and the supernatural are not so different. Metaphysical forces can be measured, in a way—if you know where to look. Energy is energy, whether it's atomic or arcane. We just need to understand how this mansion is channeling it."

The physicist frowned but nodded slightly, acknowledging the possibility, however reluctantly. "So what do we do? Find the source of this power and neutralize it?"

"That's part of it," Brandt replied. "But this mansion... it's not just a building. It's a living entity now, tied to a malevolent intelligence. We're dealing with an ancient structure, likely built on ley lines or some other source of natural power. It's been feeding on the souls trapped within it for centuries, but the blood moon amplified its abilities. We need to sever its connection to those ley lines—or whatever it's using."

Donovan's fingers drummed the table. "And how do we do that?"

Sergei's lips curled into a knowing smile. "That's where my expertise comes in. To break such a connection, you need something equally powerful. A ritual, a banishment... something that can disrupt the mansion's link to this world. But," he paused, letting his words hang ominously in the air, "such rituals require immense sacrifice. Are you willing to go that far?"

"I've seen enough men die trying to solve this with bullets. I'll do whatever it takes," Donovan said with a grim determination.

Imogen interjected, her tone sharp. "Rituals involving sacrifice are not the only way. We Wiccans believe in balance, not destruction. There are protective spells that can shield us as we approach the mansion, binding its power temporarily. But we'll need to combine forces—magick, science, and everything in between."

Eleanor sighed, rubbing her temples. "Fine. I'll concede that traditional science won't work here. But we still need a plan. I can develop something to track the energy flow—some kind of detector. If we can measure the energy, we can determine the source, whether it's ley lines or something else."

Brandt nodded. "And once we know the source, we can act. But we'll also need knowledge of the mansion's history. It didn't start with the blood moon. There's something older, darker tied to that place."

"That's why I'm here," Donovan said. "We've scoured every historical record we could find. There are references to a cult, ancient rites... but nothing concrete. We'll need someone with deeper knowledge of mythologies—someone who understands the symbols and rituals from a historical context."

Brandt tapped his chin. "Leave that to me. I'll work with Sergei to piece together the puzzle. There's always a pattern, and myths are often based in truth. The mansion's history will likely hold the key to unraveling its power."

The room grew quiet again as everyone absorbed the gravity of the situation. The team was assembled, a strange mixture of minds that had never thought they'd work together—scientists, witches, occultists, and scholars—each tasked with solving a problem beyond human understanding.

"So, what now?" Eleanor asked, looking around the table.

Donovan stood, his gaze hard and unflinching. "Now, we prepare. Each of you has a role to play. We gather intel, we gather our strength, and then we move on the mansion. This time, we won't fail."

Imogen rose as well, her voice cutting through the tension. "Remember, General, this isn't just about brute force. We are entering a place where the laws of reality bend and break. We'll need more than weapons. We'll need belief."

As the room emptied, each member of the team felt the weight of the task ahead. The Nightmare Mansion was unlike anything they had ever encountered—a malevolent force, feeding on darkness, growing stronger by the day. But now, they had a plan.

Whether it would be enough to stop the mansion's spread remained to be seen.

Chapter 2: Into the Depths

The wind howled through the dense trees surrounding the Nightmare Mansion, carrying with it an unnatural chill. The expedition team, assembled from the best minds in both science and the occult, stood before the massive iron gates that marked the threshold between the known world and the horrors beyond.

Captain Jack Johnson, a battle-hardened soldier with years of experience in hostile territory, stood at the forefront, his hand resting on the hilt of his sidearm. His sharp blue eyes scanned the mansion's decaying facade, noting the way the walls seemed to ripple in the moonlight. It was as though the structure itself was alive, breathing in the night air, waiting.

"This place..." Imogen Reed whispered, clutching the pendant around her neck. "It's thick with energy. Dark, oppressive. We should not linger."

Captain Johnson nodded but kept his focus ahead. "No one's staying behind. We're moving in as a unit, and we stay together. No exceptions."

Sergei Volkov, the dark-eyed occultist, chuckled softly from the back of the group. "Together, indeed. Let's see how long that lasts."

Johnson shot him a look. "We're all professionals here, Volkov. I don't need your commentary."

"Just stating the obvious, Captain," Sergei replied, his voice dripping with mock innocence. "This mansion has a way of... separating the wheat from the chaff, as they say."

Eleanor Blackwood, the physicist, adjusted the scanner in her hands, the small screen displaying strange energy spikes emanating from the mansion. "I'm reading massive energy fluctuations. These readings don't match anything I've seen before. We need to be cautious."

"We are cautious," Johnson replied, signaling for the team to move forward. "But we also don't have time to waste. The longer we wait, the more power this place draws."

Professor Marcus Brandt, walking beside Imogen, surveyed the mansion with wide eyes. "It's an ancient structure. The architecture isn't just Gothic—there are elements of older civilizations embedded in its design. I see symbols from Egyptian, Celtic, and even pre-Sumerian cultures. This place has been feeding on fear for millennia."

"Let's hope it doesn't feed on us next," Eleanor muttered under her breath.

The gate creaked as Captain Johnson pushed it open, the sound echoing unnaturally in the still night. Beyond lay a cobblestone path, flanked by withered trees whose branches twisted into unnatural shapes. They moved as though alive, reaching out to the team as they passed. Sergei moved his fingers subtly, muttering a warding spell, his eyes narrowing at the branches as they withdrew slightly at his command.

"Nice trick," Imogen remarked, raising an eyebrow. "But those won't be the last things we have to worry about."

"No," Sergei replied. "They're merely the welcoming committee."

The mansion loomed before them, its once-grand doors now rotted and broken. As the team approached, the air grew heavier, thick with the scent of decay and something else—something foul and unnatural, like the stench of death itself.

Captain Johnson took a deep breath, his hand gripping his weapon more tightly. "Alright, team, this is it. Stay sharp, and keep your heads on a swivel. We don't know what's waiting for us inside."

With a final glance at his team, Johnson pushed open the doors, and the group entered the Nightmare Mansion.

The moment they stepped inside, the temperature dropped several degrees, and an oppressive weight settled over them. The interior of the mansion was worse than the exterior—dust and cobwebs clung to every surface, and the walls seemed to pulse with an otherworldly energy. The air was thick with the sounds of distant whispers, though there was no sign of their source.

"We need to move quickly," Eleanor said, her eyes glued to her scanner. "The energy spikes are getting stronger. Whatever's powering this place is deep within, and we need to get to it before it grows any further."

Johnson nodded, motioning for the team to follow. "Stay close. I don't want anyone getting separated."

They moved deeper into the mansion, their footsteps echoing through the empty halls. Shadows danced along the walls, moving in ways that defied logic, as if they had a life of their own. Every now and then, one of the team members would catch a glimpse of something—something just out of sight, lurking in the corners of their vision. But when they turned to look, there was nothing there.

Imogen's voice cut through the silence, low and urgent. "This house is alive. It's feeding on our fear, growing stronger with every step we take."

"I know," Johnson replied, his voice calm but tense. "But we've got a job to do, and fear isn't going to stop us."

Suddenly, there was a crash from one of the side rooms, and the team froze. Johnson raised his hand, signaling for silence. His other hand rested on his sidearm as he moved cautiously toward the source of the noise. The rest of the team followed closely behind, their eyes scanning the darkness.

As they reached the doorway, Johnson signaled for Brandt to open it. The professor nodded, pushing the door open with a creak. Inside was a large dining room, but the once-grand table had been upended, chairs scattered and broken.

And then, out of the darkness, something moved.

A figure—twisted and grotesque, its body hunched and malformed—emerged from the shadows. Its eyes glowed with a sickly green light, and its mouth opened in a silent scream, revealing rows of jagged teeth.

"Fall back!" Johnson shouted, drawing his weapon.

But before anyone could move, the creature lunged at them with inhuman speed. Eleanor screamed as it swiped at her, barely missing by inches as she dove out of the way. Johnson fired two shots, the sound deafening in the enclosed space, but the bullets passed through the creature as though it were made of smoke.

"Magick!" Imogen shouted. "It's a wraith! Bullets won't work!"

Sergei stepped forward, his eyes blazing with dark intent as he raised his hand, chanting words in a language no one recognized. The creature howled, its form distorting as the spell took hold. With a final shriek, it dissipated into a cloud of smoke, vanishing into the ether.

The team stood in stunned silence, their breaths coming in ragged gasps. Johnson lowered his weapon, his eyes still scanning the room for any sign of the wraith's return.

"Everyone okay?" he asked, his voice steady despite the adrenaline coursing through him.

Eleanor nodded, though her face was pale. "That thing... it wasn't natural."

"Nothing in this place is," Brandt said, his voice grim. "And we've barely scratched the surface."

Johnson glanced at Sergei, who was still standing with his hand raised, his eyes locked on the spot where the wraith had disappeared. "Nice work, Volkov."

Sergei smirked, lowering his hand. "I told you, Captain. Bullets won't help you here. But magick might."

Johnson nodded, his expression hardening. "Let's keep moving. We've got a lot more ground to cover before we reach the heart of this place."

As they continued deeper into the mansion, the darkness seemed to press in around them, the very walls whispering secrets no living being should hear. Each step they took brought them closer to the heart of the Nightmare Mansion, but also deeper into its twisted, malevolent grasp.

Captain Johnson glanced back at his team, their faces tense but determined. He could only hope they'd make it out alive.

But as the mansion groaned around them, like a beast stirring from slumber, he wasn't so sure.

Chapter 3: The Wraith's Embrace

The oppressive darkness of the Nightmare Mansion seemed to grow heavier as the team pressed onward, deeper into the belly of the beast. Every creak of the floorboards, every whisper of wind through the ancient corridors sent a shiver down the spines of even the most hardened members of the group. Captain Jack Johnson led the way, his eyes focused, his grip tight on the hilt of his weapon despite knowing it would offer little defense against what lurked here.

The atmosphere was thick, like walking through water. There was something waiting, watching them from the shadows. Captain Johnson could feel it—the growing malevolence, like a storm gathering strength.

"I don't like this," Eleanor muttered, her gaze flicking nervously between her scanner and the hallway ahead. "The energy readings are spiking. It's like the mansion is reacting to us."

Sergei Volkov, ever the cynic, smirked. "Of course it's reacting. We're intruders in its domain. But don't worry, Captain Johnson is here to protect us with bullets."

Johnson shot him a warning glare. "Keep moving, Volkov. We're not stopping until we reach the heart of this place."

The rest of the team followed in silence, each step heavy with foreboding. The walls themselves seemed to close in around them, narrowing the path. Shafts of pale moonlight pierced through the cracked windows, casting eerie shadows that danced and twisted, mimicking shapes that no one dared acknowledge.

Suddenly, Imogen Reed stopped in her tracks, her hand tightening around her pendant. "Wait. Something's coming."

The team froze. Johnson turned, scanning the dimly lit hallway behind them. "What is it?" he asked, his voice low and controlled.

Imogen's face had gone pale, her eyes wide as she whispered, "A presence. Old. Hungry."

A chill ran down Johnson's spine, but he kept his voice steady. "We stay together. Nobody breaks formation."

The words had barely left his mouth when the temperature in the hallway plummeted. Frost began to creep along the walls, and the air filled with an unnatural stillness. From the shadows, a figure began to materialize—a wraith, its form translucent and grotesque. Its eyes glowed with an unnatural green light, and its long, skeletal fingers seemed to reach out for them.

"It's the same thing as before!" Eleanor gasped, backing away. "We need to move—now!"

But Captain Johnson stood his ground, locking eyes with the wraith. He could feel its malice, its hunger, radiating toward him like a physical force. "Everyone get back," he ordered, his voice sharp. "Volkov, Imogen—do something."

But even as he gave the command, he felt it—a tug, deep in his chest. The wraith's gaze locked onto him, and in an instant, its skeletal hand shot forward, passing through Johnson's chest like mist. His body stiffened, his eyes widening in horror as the cold spread through his veins.

"Captain!" Imogen screamed, rushing toward him, but it was too late.

The wraith's hand wrapped around Johnson's heart—not physically, but spiritually. He felt his soul being pulled from his body, drawn into the creature's grasp. His knees buckled as an intense cold flooded his body. Every breath became labored, and the world around him blurred.

Johnson tried to fight back, tried to lift his weapon or shout an order, but his strength drained from him like water slipping through his fingers. He was helpless, a mere vessel for the wraith's hunger. His comrades' voices sounded distant, distorted.

"Stay with us, Jack!" Eleanor shouted, but her voice seemed to come from miles away.

Sergei began chanting, his voice low and powerful as he tried to cast a banishment spell, but the wraith only tightened its grip, feeding off Johnson's life force with ravenous glee. Imogen was already chanting her own protective spell, her hands glowing faintly, but nothing seemed to work. The wraith was too strong.

Johnson's eyes met Imogen's for one brief, terrible moment. He tried to say something, anything, but his mouth wouldn't move. His vision darkened as the last of his strength left him, and with a final, shuddering gasp, Captain Jack Johnson fell to the floor, his once-vibrant body reduced to a lifeless husk.

"No!" Imogen dropped to her knees beside him, her hand trembling as she reached for his face. His skin was cold to the touch, his eyes wide and empty—soulless. The wraith hovered for a moment longer, its eerie gaze sweeping over the rest of the team before it dissipated into the darkness, leaving nothing behind but silence.

Eleanor stood frozen, her breath coming in shallow gasps as she looked down at Johnson's body. "He's... gone."

Sergei, who had stopped chanting, shook his head grimly. "His soul... devoured."

Imogen bowed her head, her voice thick with grief. "I should have been faster. I should've..."

"There was nothing you could have done," Brandt said, his voice shaking as he placed a hand on her shoulder. "The wraith was too powerful."

Sergei stepped forward, his expression unreadable. "He was the first. But he won't be the last."

"We can't just leave him here," Eleanor said, her voice wavering. "We have to—"

"We have to keep moving," Sergei interrupted, his voice cold and practical. "The mansion is feeding on our fear. If we don't act quickly, more will follow in his footsteps."

Imogen stood slowly, her eyes red with unshed tears. "He was a good man. He didn't deserve this."

"No one deserves what's coming," Sergei said darkly.

Captain Jack Johnson, their leader and protector, had become the first casualty of the Nightmare Mansion. His body, now an empty shell, lay crumpled on the cold stone floor as the remaining members of the team gathered around him in silent mourning. The weight of his loss hung heavy over them all, a grim reminder that none of them were safe within these cursed walls.

"We press on," Imogen said softly, her voice breaking but resolute. "For him."

The others nodded in agreement, though their faces were pale with fear and doubt. With one last glance at Johnson's lifeless form, the team gathered their courage and continued deeper into the mansion, knowing that whatever lay ahead would only grow more dangerous.

But the shadow of the wraith lingered, an omen of the darkness to come.

Chapter 4: Unseen Eyes

The silence inside the Nightmare Mansion was unbearable, pressing down on the expedition team like a tangible weight. Every step they took seemed to echo too loudly, as if the house itself were listening, absorbing their presence. After Captain Jack Johnson's death, a suffocating tension settled over the group. They moved slower, their movements cautious, their gazes constantly flickering to the shifting shadows around them.

High Priestess Sandra Emerald had been brought into the team for her unique talents. A powerful psychic and clairvoyant, she had spent years honing her ability to see beyond the veil of the physical world, to sense and communicate with the spirits that lingered in the places most people avoided. But this... this mansion was different. It was not just haunted—it was a beacon for the dead and worse. And now, Sandra could feel the weight of their attention, their unseen eyes tracking the group's every step.

"There are many spirits here," Sandra whispered, her voice barely audible in the oppressive silence.

Sergei Volkov glanced at her from the corner of his eye. "We expected that, didn't we?"

Sandra shook her head, her brow furrowed in concentration. "This is... different. It's not just the dead. It's something more. There are *eyes* on us, watching, waiting. They aren't human."

Eleanor, ever the skeptic, adjusted her equipment, glancing nervously at Sandra. "What do you mean, 'not human'? You're saying there's something else?"

Sandra's gaze remained fixed on the shadows ahead, her eyes distant, as if seeing something the rest of them could not. "Malevolent forces.

They've been here far longer than any of the human souls trapped in this place. They're ancient. Predatory."

The team halted, their eyes scanning the dimly lit corridor. The air seemed to thicken, and the shadows grew darker, more oppressive. Imogen stepped closer to Sandra, her voice a whisper. "Can you tell where they are? How close?"

Sandra closed her eyes, breathing deeply as she reached out with her senses. She could feel the spirits pressing against the edges of her mind, like invisible hands brushing her consciousness. Her skin prickled as she sensed their hunger—these spirits were not content to simply observe. They were waiting for a moment of weakness, for the team to falter.

"They're everywhere," Sandra murmured, her voice tight with concentration. "Watching us from the walls, the floors, the ceiling. They see everything we do, hear everything we say."

Sergei grunted, his tone half-joking to mask his unease. "Great. Spies in the walls. Just what we needed."

Sandra's eyes flew open, a sharp intake of breath cutting through the air. "No. These aren't spies. They're hunters."

Eleanor swallowed hard, her eyes darting around. "We can't fight what we can't see."

Sandra nodded, her face pale. "They're waiting for us to make a mistake. For one of us to fall behind, to lose focus. And then..."

Her words hung in the air, unfinished but understood. The unseen eyes were not just watching—they were calculating, waiting for the perfect moment to strike.

"We can't stay here," Imogen said, her voice firm but laced with urgency. "We need to keep moving, keep our energy strong. Sandra, can you ward us? At least slow these things down?"

Sandra closed her eyes again, focusing on the protective charms she carried. She drew a deep breath, her hands moving in intricate patterns as she whispered incantations in a language far older than any spoken by humans today. A soft, golden light flickered around the group as she worked, forming a barrier between them and the spirits lurking in the shadows.

"There," Sandra said, opening her eyes. "It won't hold them off forever, but it'll give us time."

Sergei nodded approvingly. "Good. Now we move."

As they continued through the mansion, the oppressive sensation of being watched never lifted. The walls seemed to shift subtly as they passed, their texture almost breathing. The unseen eyes followed them, and though Sandra's protective barrier held, she could still feel the spirits pressing against it, testing its strength.

"There's a presence ahead," Sandra warned, her voice barely above a whisper. "A strong one."

Sergei's eyes darkened. "Stronger than the wraith?"

Sandra nodded slowly. "Yes. Much stronger."

The hallway they had been walking down opened into a grand hall. Dusty chandeliers hung from the ceiling, their crystals catching the pale moonlight that filtered through the cracked windows. At the far end of the hall stood an enormous mirror, its surface dark and swirling, as if it contained something far more sinister than just a reflection.

"Don't get too close to that mirror," Sandra warned, her voice sharp. "It's not what it seems."

Brandt, who had been inspecting the symbols etched into the walls, looked up at the mirror with a frown. "What is it?"

Sandra's eyes narrowed as she focused on the swirling darkness within the glass. "It's a doorway. A portal to something far darker than this house. It's where the malevolent spirits are gathering, waiting for us to cross the threshold."

Sergei raised an eyebrow. "And if we do?"

"They'll devour us," Sandra said simply. "Body, mind, and soul."

Imogen stepped forward, her hand raised in a protective gesture. "Then we need to seal it. Can you do that?"

Sandra hesitated, her eyes fixed on the mirror. "I can try, but it's powerful. We may only have one chance."

"Do it," Johnson said, his voice steady despite the fear that gnawed at the edges of his mind. "We can't risk it being open any longer."

Sandra stepped forward, her heart pounding in her chest. She could feel the spirits pressing against the barrier she had created, their eyes fixed on her. As she began the ritual, the mirror's surface rippled, and the swirling darkness within it seemed to pulse in response to her words.

"Hold them off!" Sandra called, her voice strained. "I need time!"

Sergei and Imogen immediately began chanting their own protective spells, forming a second barrier around Sandra as she worked. The air in the grand hall grew colder, the malevolent spirits growing agitated, their whispers turning into wails of anger.

"I can feel them!" Eleanor shouted, her voice trembling with fear. "They're trying to break through!"

Sandra's hands shook as she focused all of her energy on sealing the portal. The mirror's surface began to crack, lines of golden light spreading across its surface. But the spirits were growing more aggressive, pressing harder against the barriers.

"Almost... there..." Sandra gasped, her voice barely audible over the rising wails of the spirits.

With a final, desperate surge of energy, Sandra completed the spell. The mirror shattered, the shards falling to the ground with a deafening crash. The wails of the spirits grew louder for a moment, before fading into silence. The oppressive weight that had filled the air lifted, and the unseen eyes that had followed them seemed to retreat.

Sandra collapsed to her knees, exhausted but alive. The mirror was gone, and for now, the spirits were held at bay.

Imogen rushed to her side, helping her to her feet. "You did it."

Sandra nodded weakly, her face pale. "For now. But they're still watching. They'll never stop watching."

As the team gathered themselves, the weight of the unseen eyes still lingered, a reminder that the Nightmare Mansion was far from finished with them.

"We need to keep moving," Sergei said, his voice grim. "The spirits may have pulled back, but they'll come again. And next time, they won't wait."

Sandra looked up, her eyes full of determination despite her exhaustion. "Then we'll be ready."

But as they moved deeper into the mansion, one thing became clear—no matter how powerful their wards, how strong their spells, the unseen eyes would never stop watching.

Chapter 5: The Ghosts' Wrath

The cold within the Nightmare Mansion had become unbearable, sinking into the bones of the remaining team as they ventured deeper into its labyrinthine halls. The air carried a sense of foreboding so thick it weighed on their minds, making it difficult to think clearly. Sandra Emerald, despite her earlier triumph in sealing the mirror, felt a growing unease tugging at her senses. The unseen eyes from before were no longer just watching; they were following.

The group moved cautiously through a corridor lined with faded portraits, the faces in the paintings twisted as though in eternal torment. Sandra's footsteps faltered. She had been leading the way, her psychic senses heightened, but something was wrong. The air felt different, sharper, filled with the scent of something rotten—something dead.

"We need to stop," Sandra said, her voice barely more than a whisper.

Imogen, who had been walking beside her, turned, concerned. "What is it? Do you sense something?"

Sandra's eyes narrowed as she scanned the darkness ahead. "There's... hatred. It's palpable. I can feel it in the walls, in the floor... Something is coming."

Sergei smirked darkly from the back of the group. "What now? Another spirit? Or are we dealing with more wraiths?"

Sandra shook her head. "No. Worse. Ghosts. Vengeful ones." She swallowed hard, her voice tight with tension. "They hate witches."

At that, Sergei's expression shifted, the smirk wiped clean. Imogen's face paled. "Witches? Why witches?"

Before Sandra could answer, a cold gust of wind surged through the corridor, blowing out their flashlights. Darkness enveloped them completely. Eleanor cursed under her breath as she fumbled with her equipment, trying to reignite the lights, but the oppressive cold seemed to drain the battery instantly.

In the pitch black, Sandra's heart raced. Her breath came in shallow gasps. She could feel them now—malevolent, ancient spirits drawn to her like moths to a flame, their anger a living force that wrapped around her. They had waited for this moment, waited for her to lead the group too far into the mansion's dark heart.

"They're here," she whispered, her voice trembling.

And then, out of the darkness, they came.

The first to appear was a specter—a ghostly figure clothed in tattered robes, its eyes burning with hatred. It hovered above the ground, its skeletal hand reaching out toward Sandra. But it wasn't alone. More spirits materialized behind it, their forms flickering in and out of existence, their faces twisted in fury and pain. Their voices rose, a cacophony of whispered curses and screams that echoed through the corridor.

"They were witches once," Imogen whispered, stepping back. "They must've been wronged by their own kind..."

"They're beyond reason now," Sergei said grimly. "They want revenge."

Sandra raised her hands, trying to call upon her protective wards, her voice trembling as she began to chant. But the ghosts moved too quickly. One darted forward, slashing at her with clawed fingers that tore through her protective barrier like tissue paper.

"No!" Imogen screamed, rushing toward her.

But Sandra couldn't hold them off. The spirits swarmed her, surrounding her like a pack of wolves closing in on prey. She tried to fight back, her voice rising as she cast spell after spell, but the ghosts were relentless. Their fury was too great, their hatred too consuming. One ghost, its face twisted into a grotesque mask of anger, reached out, its hand forming into a spectral blade.

Sandra's eyes widened in terror as the ghost's hand slashed across her throat, the cold of the blade so intense it burned. She gasped, her hands flying to her neck, but it was already too late. The warmth of her blood spilled between her fingers, staining the floor beneath her.

"Sandra!" Imogen screamed, her voice echoing in the hallway.

But there was nothing anyone could do. The ghosts' attack had been precise, vengeful. Sandra staggered backward, her knees buckling beneath her. Her vision blurred as she fell to the ground, her body convulsing in its final moments of life.

Imogen and Sergei rushed forward, but the ghosts had already retreated, leaving Sandra's lifeless form behind as their warning. The spirits had exacted their vengeance. Her body lay crumpled on the cold stone floor, her eyes wide open, staring into nothingness.

Eleanor stood frozen in shock, her mind reeling from the suddenness of the attack. "She's gone..." she whispered, her voice hollow.

Imogen knelt beside Sandra's body, tears streaming down her face. "She tried to warn us," she said, her voice thick with emotion. "She knew they were coming."

Sergei stood silently, his face grim. He had seen death before, but this... this was different. The mansion had taken another of their own, and the ghosts had made their message clear: no witch would be allowed to leave alive.

"We need to keep moving," Sergei said coldly, his voice cutting through the silence. "Sandra's death won't be the last if we don't finish what we came here to do."

Imogen glared at him, her grief quickly turning to anger. "You don't care at all, do you?"

Sergei's dark eyes met hers, devoid of any emotion. "I care about survival. We can mourn later—if we live."

Eleanor nodded reluctantly. "He's right. We can't stay here."

Imogen looked down at Sandra's still form, her heart breaking. She reached out, gently closing her friend's eyes before standing. "Let's go," she said, her voice barely above a whisper. "But we won't forget her."

The team gathered their courage and pressed on, but the weight of Sandra's death hung over them like a dark cloud. The ghosts had struck swiftly and without mercy, leaving behind only fear and loss. And as the group continued deeper into the Nightmare Mansion, one thing became certain—the spirits would not rest until they had claimed every last soul.

As they disappeared into the shadows of the next corridor, Sandra's body lay behind them, a grim reminder of the ghosts' wrath, her throat slit in a brutal act of vengeance. The mansion had claimed another life, and it would not be the last.

Chapter 6: Echoes of the Past

The team moved cautiously, the loss of Sandra weighing heavily on their hearts, though none voiced their grief aloud. The corridors of the Nightmare Mansion seemed to stretch endlessly, twisting and turning in ways that defied logic. Shadows danced on the walls, their shapes shifting like phantoms. There was a constant, oppressive sense of being watched, a feeling that something ancient and malevolent lingered just out of sight, waiting for the right moment to strike.

Steven Johnson, the team's mythology expert, walked at the rear of the group, his keen eyes scanning every inch of the mansion's architecture. He had been quiet since they entered, absorbed in the patterns and symbols that lined the walls, floors, and even the ceilings. His mind raced, trying to piece together the fragmented history of this cursed place.

"Steven," Imogen called softly from ahead, her voice breaking his concentration. "You've been staring at the walls for an hour. What are you seeing?"

Steven blinked, tearing his gaze from the faded carvings on the wall and hurrying to catch up with the others. "There's something more to this place," he said, his voice steady but laced with excitement. "These symbols—they're not just decorative. They're telling a story."

"A story about what?" Eleanor asked, her skepticism barely concealed as she adjusted the energy scanner in her hands.

Steven paused, his fingers lightly tracing one of the carvings. "This mansion is older than we thought. Much older. I've seen symbols from several ancient civilizations, but none of them should be here. Egyptian, Babylonian, Sumerian—they're all woven into the fabric of this place. And it's not just random. These hieroglyphs, these carvings—they point to something... divine."

Sergei scoffed from the back, his arms crossed. "Divine? You mean another ghost story?"

"No," Steven said sharply, his eyes narrowing. "I mean forgotten gods. Deities lost to time, erased from history. This place is tied to them, somehow."

Imogen looked at him, intrigued. "Go on."

Steven took a deep breath and continued, his eyes glowing with the passion of his discovery. "Look here," he said, pointing to a series of hieroglyphs etched into the stone wall beside them. "These markings—this one in particular—it's an ancient symbol representing the god Anpu, or Anubis. But next to it... this is something else. Something I don't recognize from any known pantheon."

Eleanor stepped closer, squinting at the hieroglyphs. "I'm no expert, but that doesn't look like any Egyptian carving I've seen."

"Exactly," Steven said, excitement growing in his voice. "It's similar to Anubis, but not identical. This is a depiction of a deity that predates even the Egyptians' concept of death. This place, this mansion—it's not just cursed. It's a temple. A shrine to gods that have been forgotten by the world."

Sergei let out a derisive chuckle. "Gods? We're dealing with spirits, not gods, Johnson."

Steven's expression hardened. "Spirits and gods aren't as different as you might think, Volkov. What we're dealing with here—these aren't ordinary ghosts. They're manifestations of something far older and more powerful. This mansion is alive because it's feeding off the energy of these forgotten deities."

Imogen shivered, rubbing her arms. "What kind of gods would need a place like this?"

"Gods of death, chaos, and destruction," Steven said, his voice dropping to a whisper. "Deities that demanded sacrifice. There are legends, old ones, about gods who were worshipped through blood and death, who thrived on fear. This mansion is their sanctuary, their tomb, and perhaps even their prison."

Eleanor's face paled slightly. "So... this place isn't just haunted. It's being fueled by ancient, forgotten gods."

"Exactly," Steven nodded, his fingers tracing another set of carvings. "The blood moon, the wraiths, the spirits—it's all connected to their return. The more death and fear this place absorbs, the stronger they become."

Imogen frowned, her voice barely above a whisper. "Is there any way to stop them? Can we banish these... deities?"

Steven hesitated, his brow furrowing. "I don't know. There are no surviving records of anyone successfully dealing with these kinds of beings. But there might be something here—something in the mansion's history, buried in these hieroglyphs. If we can decipher them fully, we might find a way."

"Great," Sergei said sarcastically. "We just need to translate ancient hieroglyphs in the middle of a haunted mansion while malevolent spirits pick us off one by one. Simple."

Eleanor ignored his cynicism, turning to Steven with urgency. "Is there anything else you can make out from these hieroglyphs? Something we can use now?"

Steven stepped back from the wall, studying the symbols intently. His heart raced as his eyes traced the lines, connecting pieces of a forgotten history. "There's more here," he muttered to himself, barely loud enough for the others to hear. "A ritual... a binding."

Imogen leaned in closer. "A binding? What kind of binding?"

Steven's eyes widened as he realized the significance of the carvings. "It's a binding ritual. The mansion itself is bound to these deities—it's drawing power from them. But if we can reverse the ritual, we might be able to sever that connection. It wouldn't destroy the mansion, but it would cut off its source of power."

Eleanor looked at him, hope flickering in her eyes. "So we could weaken the mansion? Stop it from expanding?"

Steven nodded. "It's possible. But we'd need to perform the ritual in the heart of the mansion, where the connection is strongest."

"And what does that entail?" Imogen asked cautiously.

Steven hesitated again. "Blood," he said quietly. "The original ritual was performed with blood. Sacrifice. It may require the same."

Imogen's face tightened, and Eleanor's expression hardened. "So we'll need to offer a sacrifice," she said flatly.

Sergei stepped forward, his voice cold and practical. "Then we do what we must. I don't care what it takes. We sever this connection, or we die here."

The team fell silent, the weight of Steven's discovery pressing down on them. The realization that they were not merely dealing with spirits but forgotten gods bent on destruction sent a ripple of fear through them all. They had thought the wraiths and ghosts were the worst of it. They were wrong.

Steven stepped back from the wall, his eyes filled with a quiet determination. "We need to find the heart of the mansion. That's where the ritual was performed. That's where we'll break the connection."

Imogen nodded, though her face was pale. "Then we go deeper. No turning back."

Sergei chuckled darkly. "Deeper into the belly of the beast. I hope you're all prepared for what we'll find."

With that grim thought hanging in the air, the group pressed on, deeper into the mansion. The walls closed in around them, the shadows lengthening as they ventured further into the unknown. And though none of them spoke of it, they all felt the eyes watching them once more—the unseen gaze of forgotten deities, waiting for their time to rise again.

Chapter 7: Encounter with Chaos

The oppressive weight of the mansion seemed to grow heavier with each step the group took. The deeper they ventured, the more the air itself felt charged with something ancient, something primal. Shadows writhed on the walls, and every so often, a faint whisper could be heard, though none of them dared to listen too closely. Steven Johnson, his mind still racing from the discovery of the ancient hieroglyphs, walked at the front of the group now, his eyes darting between the symbols etched into the walls, trying to piece together the fragments of forgotten history.

"We're getting close," Steven muttered, more to himself than the others. "The energy is almost overwhelming."

Imogen, walking beside him, glanced at him warily. "Close to what, exactly?"

Steven turned to her, his expression unreadable. "To the heart of this place. To where the ritual was performed. But more than that—something is waiting for us. Something... ancient."

Sergei, ever the cynic, scoffed. "You sound like you're looking forward to it."

Steven gave a dark smile. "Not exactly. But as a scholar of mythology, this is... unprecedented. These deities—forgotten for thousands of years—are alive here, feeding on the fear, the chaos."

Eleanor looked over her shoulder, her voice taut with tension. "I just hope your curiosity doesn't get us all killed, Johnson."

They continued forward, the corridor opening into a vast, dimly lit chamber. The air was thick with dust, and the walls were adorned with carvings and murals depicting scenes of chaos—storms, battles, and destruction on an apocalyptic scale. At the far end of the chamber stood an altar, its surface cracked and stained with something dark and ancient.

Steven's breath caught in his throat as his eyes scanned the altar. There, carved into the stone, was the unmistakable form of an Egyptian deity. The head of a strange creature with long, squared ears and a body that radiated power and malevolence.

"Seth," Steven whispered, his voice barely audible. "The Egyptian god of chaos."

Imogen looked at him sharply. "Seth? As in... the Seth?"

Steven nodded, stepping closer to the altar, his eyes wide with awe. "Yes. The god of storms, disorder, and violence. He was the enemy of order and creation—worshiped by those who thrived in chaos. I've read stories about him, but this..."

Sergei's eyes narrowed as he studied the altar. "Why would an Egyptian god be connected to this place?"

"It's not just this place," Steven said, his voice filled with excitement. "It's the mansion's very foundation. Seth is at the core of it—he is the chaos that feeds this house. The blood moon, the wraiths, the spirits—they're all manifestations of his power."

Imogen frowned, stepping closer to Steven. "So if Seth is the source of the chaos, how do we stop him?"

Before Steven could answer, the air in the chamber shifted. A low rumble echoed through the room, and the shadows seemed to twist unnaturally, pulling toward the altar. The temperature dropped suddenly, and a figure began to materialize in the center of the room, coalescing from the darkness itself.

It was Seth.

The god of chaos stood before them, his towering form cloaked in shadow. His body was humanoid, but his head was that of a strange, jackal-like beast, his eyes glowing with a terrible red light. He radiated power, his presence overwhelming, suffocating.

Steven froze, his heart hammering in his chest. He had studied gods his entire life, read stories of their wrath and their power, but nothing could have prepared him for this. This was not a mere spirit or apparition—this was a god, ancient and terrible, a force of chaos given form.

"Seth," Steven whispered, unable to tear his eyes away from the figure.

The god's glowing eyes flicked toward Steven, and a chilling smile spread across his beastly face. "You speak my name," Seth said, his voice a deep, resonant growl that seemed to vibrate through the walls. "Do you know what that means, mortal?"

Steven's throat went dry. He couldn't move, couldn't speak. He was paralyzed by the god's presence, his mind racing as he tried to comprehend the gravity of the situation.

Imogen, sensing the danger, stepped forward, her voice shaking. "Steven, get away from him! We need to go!"

But Steven didn't move. He was transfixed, locked in place by Seth's gaze. His voice, trembling, finally escaped his lips. "You... you're real."

Seth's laughter echoed through the chamber, a sound that sent shivers down the spines of everyone present. "Real?" he mused, stepping closer to Steven, his towering form casting a long shadow. "I am chaos. I am the storm that sweeps across the land. I am the destruction that brings the world to its knees. And you, mortal, dared to invoke my name."

Sergei moved forward, muttering an incantation under his breath, but Seth's gaze flicked toward him, silencing the words in his throat. The god's attention returned to Steven, who stood frozen in fear and awe.

"You sought knowledge," Seth continued, his voice a deadly whisper. "And now, you shall pay the price for it."

Before anyone could react, Seth reached out with one massive, clawed hand, his fingers curling around Steven's throat. The mythology expert gasped, his eyes widening in terror as the god's grip tightened. Seth's red eyes glowed brighter, and an eerie hum filled the air as the god's power surged.

"No!" Imogen screamed, rushing forward, but Sergei grabbed her arm, holding her back.

"We can't stop him," Sergei said grimly, his eyes locked on the horrifying scene unfolding before them.

Seth's smile widened, his voice a growl of pure malice. "You sought the truth, mortal. Now feel the chaos."

With a sickening crunch, Seth's hand twisted, and Steven's body shuddered violently. His skin began to wither, his flesh cracking and crumbling as if time itself was devouring him. His screams echoed through the chamber, but there was no escaping the god's grip.

In moments, Steven's body began to disintegrate, his flesh turning to dust, his bones crumbling into ash. His eyes, wide with terror, met Imogen's for the briefest moment before they, too, dissolved into nothingness.

And then, with a final, shattering scream, Steven Johnson was gone.

The dust that had once been his body scattered across the floor, and Seth's dark laughter filled the chamber once more. The god of chaos stepped back, his glowing red eyes gleaming with satisfaction as he surveyed the group.

"Let this be a lesson," Seth growled, his voice filled with dark amusement. "You do not invoke the name of chaos without paying the price."

Imogen fell to her knees, tears streaming down her face as she stared at the pile of ash that had once been her friend. Sergei stood silently beside her, his expression cold and unreadable. Eleanor, shaken to her core, could barely contain her fear.

Seth's form began to fade, his voice echoing in the chamber as he disappeared into the shadows. "Chaos reigns in this place, mortals. And you will not escape it."

And then he was gone, leaving the team alone in the dark, with only the echo of his laughter and the ashes of their fallen comrade to remind them of the wrath of chaos.

Chapter 8: The Celestial Gate

The remaining team was reeling after the horrifying death of Steven Johnson. His ashes still lingered in the air, a haunting reminder of the god of chaos they had faced. Samantha Carter, the team's astrophysics expert, stood at the rear, her mind grappling with the sheer impossibility of everything they had encountered. Her rational, scientific approach to life had been shattered by the events within the Nightmare Mansion. And yet, there was something else—something that pulled at the edges of her mind. A cosmic anomaly that made no sense, even in the twisted reality of this place.

"We need to move," Sergei said grimly, his voice snapping Samantha from her thoughts. "Whatever that thing was, it's still watching us."

Imogen nodded numbly, her eyes still red from the loss of Steven. "I agree. We can't stay here. But where do we go?"

Samantha's gaze shifted to the ancient carvings on the walls. Her mind, trained in understanding the universe's deepest mysteries, was picking up on something—something strange, beyond the supernatural forces they'd encountered so far.

"There's something..." she muttered, almost to herself.

Sergei raised an eyebrow. "Something what? Spit it out."

Samantha stepped forward, her eyes narrowed in concentration as she studied the walls more closely. "I've been trying to reconcile everything we've seen here with what I know about astrophysics, and... there's a pattern. The symbols, the layout of the rooms—it all aligns with something."

Eleanor frowned, stepping closer. "Aligns with what? The laws of physics don't apply here."

"Exactly," Samantha said, her voice gaining strength. "That's what's bothering me. The laws of physics shouldn't apply, but they do in a very specific way. The energy signatures I've been detecting are fluctuating like a cosmic anomaly—a gravitational anomaly, to be precise. It's as if space is warping inside the mansion."

Sergei's face twisted in skepticism. "You're saying this place is a black hole now?"

"Not a black hole," Samantha corrected, "but close. It's more like a tear in the fabric of space-time. I don't think this mansion exists entirely in our reality. It's connected to something... beyond."

Imogen, trying to shake off the grief weighing her down, looked at Samantha, a glimmer of hope in her eyes. "Could it be a way out?"

Samantha hesitated. "It might be. Or it could be something far more dangerous."

Eleanor shook her head, clearly skeptical. "A cosmic anomaly inside a haunted mansion? You're reaching, Sam."

"No, I'm not," Samantha said firmly. "I've been monitoring the energy readings ever since we got here, and they've been spiking in specific locations—like there's a rift or portal. Something is distorting reality itself, and that's why none of this makes sense."

Sergei crossed his arms, unimpressed. "And where is this so-called anomaly?"

Samantha turned and pointed to the far end of the chamber. "It's through there."

The team followed her gaze to an archway that led into another corridor, one that seemed to shimmer slightly, as if the space beyond it was unstable. A low, humming sound, almost imperceptible, filled the air.

"That's where the distortion is strongest," Samantha said, her voice steady but laced with uncertainty. "I've never seen anything like this before. It's as if the very fabric of space-time is... unraveling."

Imogen swallowed, her eyes darting between Samantha and the corridor. "And you think this could be some sort of... gate?"

Samantha nodded. "A celestial gate. If I'm right, this anomaly could connect us to another dimension, or perhaps another part of the universe altogether. It's impossible to say without closer examination, but whatever's on the other side... it's not from this world."

Eleanor looked uneasy. "We don't know what's on the other side. It could be worse than what's here."

Sergei chuckled darkly. "It's hard to imagine worse than Seth."

"Maybe it's an exit," Samantha offered, though she knew the hope was thin. "Or at least, it could give us answers. This place, the mansion, is warping because of this anomaly. If we can understand it, we might be able to stop it."

Sergei narrowed his eyes, stepping closer to the shimmering archway. "Or we might unleash something even more powerful. Ever think of that?"

Samantha hesitated. "It's a risk, yes. But we're running out of options. And whatever is behind this, it's tied to the very forces that are keeping this mansion alive. If we can find a way to disrupt it, we could cripple the mansion's power."

Imogen glanced at the archway, fear and hope battling in her eyes. "Then what do we do?"

Samantha took a deep breath, her heart pounding as she weighed the decision. Every instinct as a scientist screamed at her to investigate, to push the boundaries of knowledge, to understand what no human had ever encountered before. But she knew the risks. The mansion was already dangerous, and this anomaly could be far worse.

"I'll go first," Samantha said, her voice quiet but resolute.

Sergei raised an eyebrow. "Brave, aren't we?"

"It's not bravery," Samantha replied, her eyes locked on the swirling distortion. "It's necessity. I understand the physics behind this better than anyone. If something goes wrong, I might be able to fix it."

Eleanor's expression softened slightly. "Be careful, Sam."

Samantha nodded, her mind racing as she stepped toward the archway. The air felt different here, heavier, as if the laws of reality were bending. She could feel the anomaly, a pulse of energy that tugged at her, pulling her forward. She paused at the threshold, glancing back at the others.

"If I don't make it back," she began, but Imogen cut her off.

"You will. Just... come back, okay?"

With a final nod, Samantha stepped through the archway and into the unknown.

The world around her shifted instantly. The walls of the mansion blurred, the ground beneath her feet trembling as if reality itself was unstable. The air hummed with energy, and she could feel the pull of something immense, something cosmic. It was as if she were standing on the edge of a black hole, teetering between worlds.

Her vision flickered, and suddenly, she saw it—an immense vortex of swirling light and darkness, suspended in the middle of the room. The anomaly pulsed with power, distorting space and time around it. It was beautiful and terrifying all at once, a gateway to the unknown.

Samantha's breath caught in her throat. "This... this is impossible," she whispered to herself.

But even as she marveled at the sight, she felt a rising dread. The energy coming from the vortex was not just a tear in space-time—it was alive. Something was on the other side, something vast and incomprehensible. And it was reaching out, searching for a way through.

The vortex pulsed again, and Samantha stumbled backward, realizing with sudden horror what she had uncovered.

"It's not a gate," she whispered, her voice trembling. "It's a beacon."

And whatever had heard the call was coming.

Panicked, Samantha turned and sprinted back toward the archway. The vortex roared behind her, the energy swirling more violently as she crossed the threshold back into the mansion.

She stumbled into the room, breathless, her face pale. "We need to leave," she gasped, her voice frantic.

"What did you see?" Sergei demanded, stepping forward.

Samantha shook her head, fear in her eyes. "It's not a way out. It's a beacon—something out there is responding to it. And it's coming."

The team stood frozen for a moment, the weight of her words sinking in.

"Then we have no time," Imogen said urgently. "We need to stop it. Now."

Samantha nodded, her mind racing as she tried to think of a way to close the vortex, to sever the connection before whatever was on the other side could break through.

"We'll have to destroy it," Samantha said, her voice steady despite the terror gnawing at her. "But we'll need to act fast. This anomaly is tearing the fabric of reality apart. If we don't stop it soon, the mansion won't be the only thing consumed."

With that, the team gathered their resolve, preparing to face whatever horrors lay ahead. The celestial gate had been opened, and now, they had to close it before the nightmare that had already claimed so much took the rest of their world with it.

Chapter 9: Flesh and Bone

The oppressive atmosphere in the Nightmare Mansion seemed to deepen as Samantha Carter's discovery weighed on the group's minds. The anomaly, the celestial gate, was more than they had bargained for—it was a beacon, calling out to something vast and monstrous from beyond. Tension ran high, each member of the team silently grappling with the terror of what might come through. But none of them had expected what came next.

Samantha, though shaken, moved with urgency as she led the way through another corridor. Her mind raced with possible ways to close the gate, but each solution felt more dangerous than the last. She needed time to think, but time was a luxury they didn't have.

The hallway grew colder, a sharp, unnatural chill that made the hairs on the back of her neck stand up. She slowed her pace, her breath visible in the icy air. "Does anyone else feel that?" she asked, her voice strained.

Imogen frowned, glancing around. "It's freezing in here. That can't be a good sign."

Sergei, walking a few paces behind, grunted in agreement. "It feels like something's watching us again."

Eleanor looked down at her scanner, her brow furrowing. "I'm getting strange readings. It's like the anomaly is warping everything around us—space, temperature... even time."

Samantha nodded, though her eyes never left the shadows ahead. "Stay close," she said, her voice barely above a whisper. "Something's not right."

As they moved forward, the temperature continued to drop, and a strange, foul odor filled the air—a rancid smell, like rotting meat mixed with something more animalistic. It was thick, almost suffocating.

And then, in the distance, they heard it—a low, guttural growl that reverberated through the hallway.

Samantha's heart skipped a beat. "What was that?"

Before anyone could answer, a shadow shifted at the end of the corridor. The team froze, their eyes locked on the darkness. Slowly, something emerged from the gloom—twisted, emaciated figures with elongated limbs and sunken, hollow eyes. Their skin was stretched tight over skeletal frames, their mouths wide and filled with sharp, jagged teeth. Wendigos.

"Run," Samantha whispered, her voice tight with fear.

But it was too late. The Wendigos moved with terrifying speed, their eyes glowing with a feral hunger as they closed in on the group. Samantha turned to flee, but one of the creatures was already upon her, its skeletal hand grabbing her arm with inhuman strength.

"No!" she screamed, struggling to break free, but the Wendigo's grip was like iron.

Imogen and Sergei turned, trying to cast protective spells, but the creatures were too fast. Another Wendigo lunged at Samantha, its claws raking across her back, tearing through her jacket and into her flesh. The pain was excruciating, but worse was the terror that gripped her heart.

"They're too strong!" Imogen cried, her voice panicked as she tried to summon a spell.

Samantha's vision blurred with pain as the Wendigos dragged her to the ground. She kicked and thrashed, desperate to break free, but the creatures were relentless. One of them bit into her leg, its teeth sinking deep into her flesh. The agony was unbearable, and Samantha screamed, her voice echoing through the corridor.

"Help her!" Eleanor shouted, rushing forward, but Sergei grabbed her arm, holding her back.

"There's nothing we can do," Sergei said, his voice cold but grim. "She's gone."

"No!" Imogen screamed, tears streaming down her face as she watched in horror.

The Wendigos swarmed Samantha, their emaciated bodies moving with a feral frenzy. Their claws tore into her skin, peeling away flesh in gruesome strips. Blood splattered across the stone floor, and Samantha's screams became choked gasps as the creatures ripped into her, feeding on her with savage hunger.

Her vision blurred as she felt her body being torn apart. The pain was so intense, so overwhelming, that it no longer felt real. She could hear the wet sounds of the Wendigos feasting on her, their growls and snarls filling the air as they consumed her flesh.

Imogen's sobs echoed in the distance, but Samantha could no longer see her. Her world had become a haze of agony and darkness.

And then, slowly, the pain began to fade. Her body went numb, and her vision dimmed as she slipped into the void. Her last thought was of the celestial gate, the beacon she had discovered, and the horror that would follow.

With a final, shuddering breath, Samantha Carter was gone—her body reduced to a lifeless, mangled husk, consumed by the Wendigos in a gruesome feeding frenzy.

Imogen turned away, her body trembling with sobs, unable to watch any longer. Sergei stood beside her, his expression hard as he muttered a quiet prayer.

Eleanor, pale and shaken, whispered, "She didn't deserve that."

"No one does," Sergei replied, his voice low. "But we keep moving. If we stop, we die."

Imogen wiped her tears, her heart broken but her resolve hardening. "Then we end this. For Samantha."

The group pressed on, leaving Samantha's remains behind as a grisly reminder of the mansion's horrors. The Wendigos, their hunger briefly sated, retreated into the shadows, waiting for their next victim.

But the celestial gate still loomed ahead, and the darkness of the Nightmare Mansion had yet to reveal its final, terrifying secret.

Chapter 10: Atomic Shadows

The loss of Samantha weighed heavily on the group as they ventured deeper into the bowels of the Nightmare Mansion. Each member was haunted by her screams, by the brutal image of the Wendigos tearing her apart. But there was no time for grief, not in a place like this. The mansion was alive with a malignant energy, and every step they took was a step closer to whatever lay at its heart.

Ashley Morris, an atomic engineer who had joined the team to study the strange energy signatures surrounding the mansion, lagged slightly behind the group. Her handheld radiation scanner buzzed softly, the numbers flashing on the small screen fluctuating wildly. The radiation levels within the mansion had been sporadic since their arrival, but now they were surging, spiking to dangerous levels.

"This doesn't make sense," Ashley muttered, her brow furrowed as she studied the readings.

Imogen, still shaken but trying to maintain her focus, glanced back at her. "What doesn't?"

Ashley frowned, her eyes fixed on the device. "The radiation. It's all over the place—like it's... moving."

Sergei, ever the cynic, raised an eyebrow. "Radiation doesn't move, Morris. Not like that."

"No," Ashley agreed, "not like this. It shouldn't behave like this at all." She tapped the scanner, the numbers jumping again. "There's a pattern here, but it's not random. It's almost as if it's being controlled, or at least directed."

Eleanor, whose nerves were already frayed, glanced at the engineer. "Controlled radiation? Are you saying someone—or something—is doing this intentionally?"

"I don't know," Ashley said, her voice edged with frustration. "But something is generating these spikes, and whatever it is, it's not natural. The levels we're seeing should be lethal, but they're concentrated in specific areas—pockets of extreme radiation that dissipate almost immediately. It's like shadows."

"Shadows of radiation?" Imogen asked, her brow furrowing. "How is that possible?"

Ashley hesitated, her mind racing as she tried to piece together the fragments of information she had gathered. "It's almost as if the radiation is being manipulated by an external force—something within the mansion. And it's not just background radiation—it's atomic, like fallout from a reactor or a nuclear event."

Sergei's eyes darkened. "Fallout? Are you saying this place has been hit by something nuclear?"

Ashley shook her head. "No, not exactly. But it's something similar. There are residual traces of isotopes that shouldn't be here—cesium, iodine, even plutonium. It's as if the mansion has absorbed the energy from past events, like it's drawing power from every destructive force that's ever occurred near it."

Imogen's face paled. "Like an atomic bomb?"

Ashley nodded slowly. "Yes, but more controlled. Whatever's happening here, it's been going on for centuries. The mansion is amplifying these forces, twisting them."

Eleanor stepped forward, her voice tight with concern. "Is it safe for us to even be here, then? If there's radiation, we could be poisoned."

"That's the strange part," Ashley said, glancing down at the scanner again. "The radiation should be deadly, but it's not affecting us the way it should. It's almost like it's... phasing in and out of reality. One minute it's spiking, and the next, it's gone."

Sergei snorted. "Another fun quirk of the Nightmare Mansion. What else is new?"

Ashley ignored him, her mind focused on the problem at hand. The radiation, the bizarre energy readings—none of it added up. She needed to get closer to the source, to find out what was generating these dangerous levels of atomic energy.

"There's a room ahead," Ashley said, pointing to a door at the end of the hallway. "That's where the readings are strongest. I need to see what's inside."

Imogen exchanged a wary glance with Eleanor, but nodded. "We'll go with you."

The three women moved cautiously toward the door, Sergei following at a distance, his expression unreadable. The air grew colder as they approached, the strange sense of pressure that permeated the mansion intensifying.

Ashley reached for the door handle, her hand trembling slightly. The scanner buzzed violently, the radiation levels spiking higher than they had anywhere else in the mansion. She took a deep breath and pushed the door open.

The room beyond was large and circular, its walls covered in intricate carvings and symbols that glowed faintly in the dim light. In the center of the room stood a massive, ancient machine—something that looked like a cross between a nuclear reactor and an arcane altar. Its surface was covered in wires and tubes, all of them humming with a strange, unearthly energy.

Ashley's breath caught in her throat. "This... this can't be real."

"What the hell is that?" Eleanor whispered, her eyes wide with shock.

Ashley stepped forward, her hands trembling as she held up the scanner. The radiation levels were off the charts, but more than that, she could feel the energy emanating from the machine, pulsing like a heartbeat.

"It's a reactor," Ashley said, her voice barely above a whisper. "But not like anything I've ever seen before. It's ancient, but it's still active."

Sergei scoffed from the doorway. "An ancient nuclear reactor? You expect us to believe that?"

Ashley ignored him, her mind racing as she studied the device. "It's not just a reactor. It's a conduit—channeling energy from something... else. It's drawing power from the anomaly, from the mansion itself. This is what's been causing the radiation spikes."

Imogen looked around the room, her face pale. "And what happens if it overloads?"

Ashley swallowed hard. "I don't know. But if this thing goes critical, it could take out more than just the mansion."

Eleanor's face tightened with fear. "Are you saying it's a bomb?"

"Not exactly," Ashley said. "It's more like... a battery. A massive, unstable battery that's been storing energy for centuries. But it's volatile. One wrong move, and it could release all that energy in an instant."

Sergei narrowed his eyes. "So what do we do? Shut it down?"

Ashley's mind raced as she considered their options. "I don't know if we can shut it down without triggering a meltdown. But if we can stabilize it, we might be able to stop the anomaly from growing."

Imogen nodded, her face resolute. "Then we stabilize it. Tell us what to do."

Ashley hesitated for a moment, her eyes locked on the machine. The hum of its power filled her ears, and she could feel the heat radiating from it, like standing too close to an open flame. Her instincts screamed at her to turn back, to leave this place behind, but she knew they had no choice.

"Okay," she said, her voice steady. "We need to reroute the energy flow. I can do that from here, but I'll need your help. Imogen, I need you to watch the output levels on that panel over there. If they spike too high, let me know. Eleanor, you'll monitor the cooling system—if it starts to overheat, we're in trouble."

They moved into position, their faces tense but determined. Ashley knelt beside the machine, her hands shaking as she worked. The radiation levels surged, and for a moment, she felt a wave of nausea wash over her, but she pushed it aside, focusing on the task at hand.

Minutes passed, each one feeling like an eternity. The machine groaned under the strain, its lights flickering ominously.

"Output's spiking!" Imogen shouted, her voice filled with panic.

"Cooling system's failing!" Eleanor added, her eyes wide with fear.

Ashley gritted her teeth, her fingers moving frantically over the controls. "Hold on, I'm almost there!"

Suddenly, a loud crack echoed through the room, and the machine shuddered violently. Ashley's heart stopped as she watched in horror—the machine was overloading, and there was nothing she could do to stop it.

"No!" she screamed, her hands moving faster, desperately trying to reroute the energy.

But it was too late. The machine exploded in a blinding flash of light, and the last thing Ashley saw was the room disintegrating around her, the atomic energy consuming everything in its path.

The mansion trembled, and a deafening roar filled the air as the ancient reactor unleashed its stored power. Ashley's body was vaporized in an instant, reduced to nothing but ash and atomic shadows, her final sacrifice in the battle against the horrors of the Nightmare Mansion.

Chapter 11: Infernal Flames

The mansion had become a suffocating tomb of horrors, each step dragging the survivors further into its malevolent embrace. The air was thick with an almost tangible sense of dread, and the oppressive atmosphere weighed heavily on Ashley Morris. After their harrowing encounter with the reactor-like machine and the radiation, Ashley had hoped for a brief respite—a moment to gather her thoughts and figure out their next move. But the Nightmare Mansion had no mercy left for them.

The group pressed on, the loss of Samantha and the close call with the reactor still hanging over them. Every hallway seemed to stretch endlessly, the walls covered in strange, indecipherable symbols that pulsed with a sickly glow. Ashley's mind was still racing, replaying the earlier encounter with the machine over and over. How close had they come to unleashing something catastrophic?

"I don't like this," Imogen muttered, her voice breaking through Ashley's thoughts. "It's too quiet."

Sergei scoffed. "Quiet is the least of our problems right now."

But Imogen was right—there was something unnerving about the silence. It was too complete, as if the very air was holding its breath, waiting for something to happen.

Ashley checked her radiation scanner, which had been malfunctioning ever since their encounter in the reactor room. It buzzed faintly, the numbers flickering, but the readings were erratic, like everything else in the mansion.

Suddenly, the temperature around them spiked. What had once been a cold, bone-chilling atmosphere became stiflingly hot, as if they had just stepped into the mouth of a furnace.

"What the hell?" Eleanor gasped, wiping sweat from her brow. "Why is it so hot all of a sudden?"

Ashley's skin prickled with a deep sense of foreboding. Her instincts screamed that they were no longer alone. "Something's coming," she whispered.

Imogen's hand went instinctively to the protective charms around her neck. "What is it this time?"

Before anyone could answer, a low, inhuman growl echoed from the darkness ahead. The sound was primal, guttural, like a beast stalking its prey. The shadows at the end of the corridor began to shift and move, and from them emerged a creature unlike anything Ashley had ever seen.

It was massive, towering over them with leathery wings that stretched wide, their tips brushing the walls on either side. Its eyes burned a deep, fiery red, and its body was covered in rough, scaly skin that gleamed in the dim light. Its head resembled that of a goat or dragon, with long, twisted horns curling up from its skull. Its claws clicked against the stone floor as it moved closer, and the stench of sulfur filled the air.

"The Jersey Devil," Sergei muttered, his voice filled with a mixture of disbelief and grim recognition. "Of course."

Ashley felt a wave of nausea roll through her. She had heard of the Jersey Devil before—stories of a winged beast that terrorized the Pine Barrens of New Jersey—but she had never believed them. Now, standing before the very creature from legend, her disbelief was shattered.

"It's real," Imogen whispered, her voice trembling. "It's all real."

The Jersey Devil's eyes locked onto Ashley, its nostrils flaring as it took in her scent. It let out a bone-chilling screech, its wings flaring wide as it charged toward her, flames erupting from its maw.

"Run!" Ashley screamed, but the words barely left her mouth before the creature was upon her.

The Jersey Devil moved with terrifying speed, its wings carrying it across the room in a single bound. Ashley tried to dive out of the way, but the beast's claws caught her, sending her sprawling to the ground.

Pain shot through her body as she struggled to get up, her breath coming in ragged gasps.

Imogen and Eleanor watched in horror as the creature loomed over Ashley, its eyes glowing with malevolent fire.

"Ashley, get up!" Imogen cried, her voice breaking with panic.

But it was too late.

The Jersey Devil opened its jaws, and a torrent of searing flames erupted from its mouth, engulfing Ashley in a blaze of hellish fire. The heat was unbearable, the flames licking at her skin, consuming her in seconds. Her screams echoed through the mansion, mingling with the beast's shrieks of fury as the flames consumed her flesh.

Ashley's mind was a haze of pain and terror. She could feel her skin blistering, her flesh melting as the flames devoured her. She tried to scream, but the heat scorched her lungs, leaving her gasping for breath. Her vision blurred, and the world around her became a swirling inferno of light and agony.

Sergei took a step forward, his face grim. "There's nothing we can do," he said coldly.

Imogen sobbed, her hands trembling as she clutched her charms, powerless to save her friend.

Eleanor looked away, her face pale. "This place... it's going to kill us all."

Ashley's body convulsed as the flames continued to burn, reducing her to little more than a charred husk. The smell of burnt flesh filled the air, and the Jersey Devil let out a final screech before retreating into the shadows, its hunger momentarily sated.

When the flames finally died, only charred remains were left where Ashley had stood moments before. Her once vibrant, determined spirit had been consumed, leaving behind nothing but ashes and the haunting reminder of her brutal death.

Imogen collapsed to her knees, her sobs echoing through the hallway. "She's gone..."

Sergei stood silently, his eyes fixed on the spot where Ashley's remains still smoldered. "This mansion doesn't leave anyone untouched," he muttered.

Eleanor wiped her tears, her voice shaking. "We can't stay here. We have to keep moving."

Imogen nodded weakly, though her heart was shattered. The mansion had claimed another, and it wasn't finished yet.

As they moved on, the charred remains of Ashley Morris were left behind, a testament to the infernal flames that had claimed her life. The Jersey Devil, lurking somewhere in the darkness, had fed, but the mansion's hunger was far from sated.

Chapter 12: Celestial Alignments

The suffocating darkness within the Nightmare Mansion seemed to press in tighter with each step the group took. The air felt thick, charged with a strange energy that gnawed at their nerves. Every hallway seemed to warp and twist in impossible ways, making the mansion feel alive, as if it were a sentient being reacting to their presence. Stanley Jones, an astrologist brought in for his expertise on cosmic events, walked at the rear of the group, his brow furrowed as he studied the small, worn notebook in his hands.

Stanley had always been meticulous, someone who could track the movements of the stars with perfect precision. But what he had observed over the past few hours inside the mansion disturbed him in ways he could hardly articulate. The celestial bodies were... wrong. They weren't where they were supposed to be, not according to any chart he had ever consulted. And worse, their misalignment seemed to be amplifying the mansion's malevolent energy.

Imogen's voice broke through his thoughts. "Stanley, what are you seeing? You've been staring at that notebook for an hour."

Stanley looked up, the concern evident in his eyes. "The stars... the planets... everything is out of place."

Sergei, always the cynic, raised an eyebrow. "Out of place? The stars don't move, Jones."

"They don't move like this," Stanley snapped, his frustration evident. "This isn't natural. Something is warping the very fabric of space. The mansion... it's connected to the celestial bodies in ways we don't understand."

Imogen frowned. "What do you mean? How can the stars be tied to the mansion?"

Stanley took a deep breath, struggling to put his thoughts into words. "The mansion is feeding off cosmic alignments—planetary conjunctions, eclipses, even the phases of the moon. The blood moon, in particular, is empowering this place. It's more than just a haunted house—it's a nexus of energy, drawing power from the heavens themselves."

Eleanor, still pale from the horrors they had witnessed, looked at Stanley skeptically. "You're saying this place is using the stars for power?"

Stanley nodded, flipping through the pages of his notebook. "Yes. The mansion is aligned with celestial events in a way that defies explanation. Every major cosmic event—every eclipse, every planetary alignment—is like a surge of energy for this place. It's been feeding off them for centuries, growing stronger each time."

Sergei crossed his arms, his expression unimpressed. "You're telling us that the mansion is... what? Powered by astrology?"

"Not astrology," Stanley said sharply, his eyes gleaming with intensity. "Cosmic energy. The mansion is like a conduit for the forces that govern the universe. The stars, the planets—they're all in alignment in ways that are amplifying the mansion's malevolence. And the blood moon is the key."

Imogen's eyes widened in realization. "The blood moon. That's why everything has escalated."

"Exactly," Stanley continued, his voice rising with urgency. "The blood moon is a rare celestial event, one that heightens the energy of the universe. The mansion has been waiting for it, feeding on the alignment of the celestial bodies to unleash its full potential. This is why it's happening now."

Eleanor shook her head, clearly struggling to keep up. "So, what does that mean for us? How do we stop it?"

Stanley hesitated, glancing back at his notebook. "If we can break the mansion's connection to the celestial alignments, we might be able to weaken it. But the blood moon is still high, and the planets are in perfect alignment. It's the strongest the mansion has ever been."

Sergei snorted, his voice dripping with sarcasm. "And how exactly do we break a connection to the stars? You going to shoot the moon out of the sky, Jones?"

Stanley glared at him but remained focused. "We don't need to shoot anything out of the sky. We just need to disrupt the alignment. The mansion is drawing power from a specific conjunction of planets—if we can disrupt the flow of that energy, we can stop the mansion from feeding off it."

Imogen's brow furrowed. "How do we do that? We can't exactly move planets."

Stanley stepped closer to a large, intricately carved stone altar in the center of the room. Symbols of astrological signs and celestial bodies were etched into its surface, glowing faintly. "This," he said, pointing to the altar. "This is the key. The mansion is using this altar to channel the cosmic energy. If we destroy it, we disrupt the alignment."

Eleanor's eyes narrowed as she studied the altar. "It looks ancient. Are you sure it's even possible to destroy it?"

Stanley nodded, though his face betrayed his uncertainty. "It's the only chance we have. The altar is a focal point, a conduit for the celestial energy. If we can sever its connection to the planets and the moon, we can stop the mansion from growing any stronger."

Sergei unsheathed a ceremonial dagger from his belt. "If all we have to do is break it, then let's stop talking and do it."

Imogen placed a hand on Sergei's arm, her face serious. "It might not be that simple. This place isn't just going to let us destroy it. There's a reason this altar has lasted for centuries."

Stanley swallowed hard, knowing the truth of her words. "We need to be prepared for whatever happens once we disrupt the flow of energy. The mansion is going to fight back."

Sergei stepped forward, raising the dagger. "Let's see how much it fights when this thing is in pieces."

With a grunt, he brought the dagger down onto the surface of the altar. The moment the blade struck the stone, a deafening roar echoed through the room. The ground trembled violently, and the symbols on the altar flared with a brilliant, blinding light.

Stanley staggered back, shielding his eyes from the light. "The connection is breaking!" he shouted over the roar. "Keep going!"

Sergei struck the altar again, and the light intensified, the air around them vibrating with energy. The walls of the mansion seemed to groan in protest, and the temperature plummeted as the celestial alignment began to unravel.

But then, from the shadows, a voice emerged—a low, menacing whisper that seemed to come from the very fabric of the mansion.

"You dare disrupt the flow of the heavens?" the voice hissed. "You cannot sever the stars from their course."

Imogen's face went pale as she realized the voice was not just a manifestation of the mansion, but something far older and more powerful.

"The mansion isn't speaking," she whispered, fear in her eyes. "It's the alignment itself."

Stanley's heart raced as the realization hit him. They weren't just fighting the mansion—they were battling against cosmic forces older than time itself. The celestial alignments had been set in motion long before humanity, and disrupting them had awakened something ancient and malevolent.

"We have to finish it," Stanley said through gritted teeth. "Keep going!"

Sergei slammed the dagger into the altar one final time, and with a crack that shook the very foundation of the mansion, the stone shattered. The glowing symbols flickered and died, and the energy that had been coursing through the mansion seemed to collapse in on itself.

The light faded, and the roar ceased. For a moment, there was silence.

Stanley let out a breath he hadn't realized he'd been holding. "We did it."

But as the group began to collect themselves, the ground beneath them trembled once more. The air felt heavy, suffocating, and the shadows in the room seemed to grow darker, thicker.

"The mansion's not done," Sergei muttered, his eyes scanning the room.

Stanley looked up at the sky through a crack in the ceiling. The blood moon still hung high, casting an eerie red glow over the landscape. The stars had shifted, but the cosmic forces were still in play.

"We've weakened it," Stanley said, his voice trembling. "But it's not over. The alignment is still there, just... fractured."

Imogen's face was grim. "Then we keep going. We find the heart of this place and destroy it."

Stanley nodded, though his heart was heavy with the knowledge that they were now fighting against powers far greater than they had imagined. The celestial alignment had been broken, but the Nightmare Mansion was far from finished.

As they moved deeper into the mansion, the weight of the stars pressed down on them, a reminder that their battle was not just against the horrors within, but against the very forces that governed the universe.

Chapter 13: Cavernous Horrors

The group descended deeper into the mansion, their path winding through corridors that seemed to lead nowhere and everywhere at once. After the celestial alignment had been disrupted, there was no sense of victory—only dread. The mansion's malevolence, though weakened, continued to pulse through the walls, and the group knew it was far from defeated.

Stanley Jones walked at the front, his notebook tucked under his arm. His thoughts were consumed with what they had just done—breaking the celestial alignment and disrupting the mansion's connection to the stars. It should have weakened the malevolent force, but something still felt terribly wrong. He couldn't shake the feeling that they had merely stirred the hornet's nest, unleashing something even worse.

Imogen walked beside him, her face pale and drawn, but her resolve still firm. "We're close to the heart of it, aren't we?" she asked quietly.

Stanley nodded. "I think so. The deeper we go, the stronger the energy becomes. But..." He hesitated, glancing at the walls. "There's something else down here."

"What do you mean?" Imogen asked, her voice barely above a whisper.

Stanley frowned, his eyes scanning the darkness. "The energy is... different. It's not just the mansion. There's something older. Something lurking beneath."

Sergei, bringing up the rear, chuckled darkly. "Older than the mansion? Great. Just what we needed—more horrors."

Eleanor shot him a warning look. "Be serious, Sergei. We're not out of this yet."

Stanley stopped suddenly, raising a hand for the others to do the same. "Do you hear that?"

The group fell silent, straining to listen. From somewhere ahead came a faint, scraping sound—like claws dragging across stone. The sound echoed through the tunnels, growing louder with each passing moment.

Imogen's breath caught in her throat. "What is that?"

Stanley swallowed hard, his heart pounding in his chest. "I don't know."

They moved forward cautiously, the tunnel growing narrower and more oppressive with each step. The walls were slick with moisture, and the air was thick with the smell of damp earth and decay. Shadows seemed to move of their own accord, flickering at the edges of their vision.

The scraping sound grew louder, more distinct, until it became a chorus of movement—dozens of creatures shifting in the darkness ahead.

"There's something down here," Stanley whispered, his voice trembling. "Something alive."

Before anyone could respond, the tunnel opened into a massive cavern, its ceiling disappearing into the shadows above. The floor was uneven, littered with jagged rocks and bones—ancient remains of those who had ventured into the depths and never returned.

And then they saw them.

Lurking at the edges of the cavern, half-hidden in the darkness, were creatures that defied description. They were humanoid in shape but grotesquely deformed, their bodies twisted and hunched, their skin pale and mottled. Their eyes glowed faintly in the dim light, and their mouths were filled with sharp, jagged teeth. They moved in a strange, predatory rhythm, their claws scraping against the stone as they advanced.

"Cave-dwellers," Sergei muttered, his voice filled with disgust. "I've heard stories about them. Never thought I'd see one."

"They're real," Imogen whispered, her voice filled with horror. "They're actually real."

Stanley took a step back, his breath quickening as the creatures drew closer. "We need to leave. Now."

But it was too late.

One of the cave-dwellers let out a guttural screech, and in an instant, the creatures surged forward, moving with terrifying speed. Stanley barely had time to react before the first of them reached him, its claws slashing across his chest with brutal force.

"Stanley!" Imogen screamed, rushing toward him, but Sergei grabbed her arm, pulling her back.

"We can't help him!" Sergei shouted, his voice hard. "We need to run!"

Stanley staggered backward, blood pouring from the deep gashes across his chest. He gasped for breath, his vision blurring as the creatures swarmed him. Their claws tore into his flesh, rending it from bone with sickening ease. His screams echoed through the cavern, filled with pain and terror as the cave-dwellers descended on him in a frenzy.

Imogen struggled against Sergei's grip, tears streaming down her face. "We have to help him!"

But Stanley's fate was sealed. The cave-dwellers tore him apart, their jagged teeth sinking into his flesh as they feasted on him. His body was reduced to a mangled, bloody mess in seconds, his screams dying with him as the creatures ripped him to pieces.

Eleanor turned away, her face pale, unable to watch. "We can't stop them..."

Imogen collapsed to the ground, sobbing as Stanley's lifeless body was dragged into the shadows by the creatures. Sergei tightened his grip on her arm, pulling her to her feet.

"We need to go," Sergei said coldly. "Now."

Imogen wiped her tears, her body trembling with grief and fear. She looked at the cavern, at the bloodstains that marked where Stanley had been moments before, and nodded weakly.

The group turned and fled, their footsteps echoing through the tunnels as they raced away from the horror that had consumed Stanley. The cave-dwellers, their hunger briefly sated, retreated into the shadows, waiting for their next victim.

Stanley Jones, the man who had sought to understand the cosmic forces behind the mansion, was gone—torn apart by the monsters that lurked in its hidden depths. The group pressed on, their numbers dwindling, knowing that the mansion's horrors were far from over.

Chapter 14: The Mirror's Edge

The remaining members of the group trudged through the winding corridors of the Nightmare Mansion, their faces drawn and pale. Each of them carried the weight of the horrors they had witnessed—the brutal deaths of their friends, the malevolent power that clung to the very walls of the mansion. But none of them spoke. The silence between them was thick with unspoken dread, each of them fearing what they might face next.

Imogen walked at the front, her heart heavy with grief. Stanley's death had broken something inside her, and though she knew she had to keep going, each step felt like a weight pressing down on her soul. Sergei followed closely behind, his face hard and expressionless, as though he had already resigned himself to whatever fate awaited them. Eleanor walked beside him, her eyes constantly flickering toward the shadows, her fear barely contained.

The air grew colder as they descended further into the mansion, the walls narrowing and twisting around them like a living organism. The path ahead seemed endless, but suddenly, the corridor opened up into a vast room. In the center stood a massive, ornate mirror, its surface gleaming with an unnatural light. The frame was made of dark, twisted metal, intricately carved with strange symbols and faces frozen in expressions of agony.

Eleanor took a hesitant step forward, her gaze locked on the mirror. "What... is that?"

Sergei frowned, his eyes narrowing as he studied the object. "A trap," he said coldly. "What else would it be in this place?"

Imogen's breath hitched as she felt the pull of the mirror. It was almost hypnotic, the way its surface seemed to shimmer, beckoning them closer. "There's something about it," she whispered, her voice filled with both awe and fear.

Without thinking, she moved toward the mirror, drawn to its gleaming surface. Her reflection was faint, barely visible, but as she approached, the image began to shift. What she saw was not herself—but something far darker.

In the mirror, she saw a vision of herself standing in a cemetery, her hands covered in blood. Around her were the bodies of her friends, all slain by her own hands. The horror on her face in the reflection was unmistakable, but the dark version of her smiled—a cold, twisted smile filled with malice.

"No..." Imogen whispered, stepping back, her hands trembling. "That's not me. That's not real."

But the mirror did not relent. The dark version of her stepped closer, the bloody smile widening. *You always feared this, didn't you?* the reflection whispered, though no sound escaped the mirror. *You've always been afraid of hurting the ones you love.*

Imogen's breath came in short gasps as the vision consumed her. The scene in the mirror grew more vivid, more real. She could smell the blood, hear the muffled cries of her friends as they lay dying at her feet. She stumbled back, her heart racing in terror.

"I didn't... I wouldn't..."

Sergei grabbed her arm, pulling her away from the mirror. "It's showing you your fear," he said sharply, his voice steady but cold. "It's not real."

Imogen tore her gaze away from the mirror, her body trembling with the weight of what she had seen. But as she looked up at Sergei, she saw the same haunted expression on his face. The mirror was affecting him too.

"What do you see?" Imogen asked quietly, though part of her already knew the answer.

Sergei clenched his jaw, refusing to look back at the mirror. "It's nothing," he muttered. But his voice betrayed him.

Eleanor stepped closer to the mirror, her face pale as she watched her reflection twist and morph into something unrecognizable. Her eyes widened in horror as the scene unfolded—a version of herself kneeling before a child's grave, her hands shaking with grief. The weight of her guilt was suffocating. She watched in the mirror as her reflection wept, collapsing over the grave, whispering apologies to a child who could no longer hear them.

"No," Eleanor whispered, her voice breaking. "I did everything I could. I tried..."

The mirror showed no mercy. The scene shifted, the graveyard growing darker, the child's gravestone crumbling to dust. In its place stood the child, their face twisted in anger, accusing her of abandoning them. Eleanor's knees buckled, her hands flying to her mouth as she watched the child scream at her, their voice silent but their rage clear.

"I didn't leave you," she sobbed, her heart breaking all over again.

Sergei, his face pale, turned away from the mirror, his fists clenched. "We need to move," he growled, though his voice was strained. "This place is feeding off our fears. If we stay here, it'll tear us apart."

Imogen tried to speak, but the weight of what she had seen made her voice falter. Her mind replayed the vision over and over—the dark version of herself, the blood on her hands. She could still feel the chill of the cemetery, the smell of death clinging to her.

Sergei grabbed her arm again, pulling her away from the mirror's pull. "It's not real," he said, more forcefully this time. "Don't let it in."

Eleanor, still reeling from her vision, nodded weakly and backed away from the mirror. "What... what is this thing?"

"It's a mirror that reflects your worst fears," Sergei said darkly, his eyes narrowing as he glanced at the reflective surface. "It shows you what you're most afraid of—your past, your failures, your darkest thoughts."

Imogen shook her head, her voice trembling. "How do we fight something like this?"

Sergei's eyes darkened. "We don't. We leave it behind."

But as they turned to go, the mirror's surface shimmered again, this time revealing a twisted version of Sergei, standing alone in a field of corpses. His reflection looked up at him, its eyes cold and unfeeling.

You're afraid of becoming this, the reflection whispered. *But it's already too late.*

Sergei's face hardened, but for a moment, the weight of his guilt flickered in his eyes. "Let's go," he muttered, his voice tight with emotion.

The group turned their backs on the mirror, leaving it behind as they made their way deeper into the mansion. But even as they walked away, the images lingered in their minds—the darkest parts of themselves now exposed, their deepest fears laid bare.

The Nightmare Mansion had shown them the edges of their own souls, and none of them could escape the knowledge of what they had seen.

Chapter 15: The Labyrinth's Keeper

The winding, ever-changing corridors of the Nightmare Mansion twisted and warped as if they had a mind of their own, pulling the remaining survivors deeper into the abyss. The mansion had already claimed too many lives, and each step felt like a march toward inevitable doom. Imogen, Sergei, and Eleanor were all that was left, their nerves frayed, their hearts heavy with the weight of loss.

Sergei led the way, his jaw set in determination. His movements were mechanical, driven more by instinct than hope. Behind him, Imogen and Eleanor followed, their faces pale and gaunt. The mirror they had encountered earlier had shown them all the darkest corners of their minds, and the horrors they had faced so far seemed to be designed to break them piece by piece.

But there was something different now. The air was heavier, thicker, as if the mansion itself had grown weary of its games and was ready to reveal its final, monstrous challenge.

"We need to find an exit," Imogen said, her voice barely above a whisper, though the desperation was clear. "We can't keep wandering in circles."

Sergei didn't respond. His eyes were focused ahead, scanning the twisted architecture for any sign of escape, though deep down, he knew there would be none.

"This place doesn't want us to leave," Eleanor said, her voice trembling. "It's like it's... alive."

Sergei clenched his fists. "It can try to keep us here, but we'll find a way out. We have to."

As they continued, the hallways began to shift once more, the walls twisting and curving until they found themselves in a vast, open chamber. The ceiling disappeared into darkness above, and the walls were lined with intricate carvings that seemed to pulse with a faint, eerie light.

At the center of the room stood a massive gate, carved from stone, its surface covered in the same strange symbols they had seen throughout the mansion. It was the first thing that resembled an exit since they had entered this cursed place. But even as they approached, a deep, guttural sound echoed through the chamber, freezing them in place.

"Do you hear that?" Imogen asked, her voice tight with fear.

Sergei nodded, his hand reaching instinctively for the dagger at his belt. "Stay close," he whispered. "Something's here."

The sound grew louder, a deep, rhythmic thudding, like the footsteps of a giant. The ground trembled with each step, the vibrations shaking loose dust from the walls and ceiling. And then, from the shadows at the far end of the chamber, a monstrous figure emerged.

It stood at least twenty feet tall, its massive, hulking frame covered in thick, leathery skin. Its face was a twisted amalgamation of animal and man, with burning, red eyes and a gaping maw filled with jagged teeth. Two massive horns jutted from its skull, curving upward like those of a bull. In its hand, it carried a gigantic, rusted blade that scraped the ground as it moved.

The Labyrinth's Keeper.

Imogen took a step back, her eyes wide with terror. "What... is that?"

"The final guardian," Sergei muttered grimly. "It's been waiting for us."

Eleanor's voice trembled as she clutched the pendant around her neck. "We can't fight that."

The Keeper let out a deafening roar that shook the very foundations of the mansion. Its eyes locked onto the group, and with a single, thunderous step, it began to advance, its massive blade dragging behind it, leaving a trail of sparks in its wake.

"We have no choice," Sergei growled, his grip tightening on the dagger. "It won't let us leave."

Imogen's heart raced as the monstrous guardian approached. "We can't fight that thing! We need a plan!"

Sergei's mind raced, but the only thought that surfaced was survival. "We don't need to kill it," he said. "We just need to get past it."

The Keeper roared again, raising its massive blade as it lumbered closer. The sheer size of the creature was overwhelming, its presence filling the room with an oppressive sense of doom. It was a force of nature, ancient and unstoppable.

Sergei glanced at Imogen and Eleanor. "When I give the signal, run for the gate."

Imogen's eyes widened. "What are you going to do?"

Sergei didn't answer. He took a deep breath, steeling himself for what was about to come. "Stay behind me," he ordered, his voice firm. "When I say go, you go."

Before they could argue, the Keeper lunged forward, its massive blade swinging in a deadly arc. Sergei threw himself to the side, narrowly avoiding the blow as the blade crashed into the ground, sending stone and dust flying into the air.

"Now!" Sergei shouted, his voice cutting through the chaos.

Imogen and Eleanor didn't hesitate. They sprinted toward the gate as the Keeper's attention shifted toward them. The monster's eyes burned with fury as it turned, raising its blade for another strike.

Sergei gritted his teeth, rushing forward and slashing at the creature's leg with his dagger. The blade barely pierced the thick hide, but it was enough to draw the Keeper's attention back to him.

"Over here, you ugly bastard!" Sergei shouted, dodging another swing of the massive sword.

The Keeper roared in rage, its bloodshot eyes locked onto Sergei as it raised its blade high. But before it could strike, Imogen and Eleanor reached the gate, their hands fumbling with the strange symbols carved into the stone.

"Hurry!" Sergei shouted, ducking as the blade narrowly missed his head.

Imogen's hands shook as she traced the symbols on the gate, trying to make sense of them. "I don't know how to open it!"

Eleanor's voice was filled with panic. "There has to be a way! Keep trying!"

Sergei's heart raced as the Keeper loomed over him, its eyes glowing with murderous intent. He could feel the exhaustion setting in, his body slowing under the relentless assault of the creature. He knew he couldn't keep this up for much longer.

"Imogen!" he shouted. "Now would be a good time!"

Finally, Imogen's fingers pressed down on a symbol that seemed to glow brighter than the rest. There was a deep rumble, and the gate began to creak open, the stone grinding against itself as the ancient mechanism activated.

"It's opening!" Imogen cried, her voice filled with relief.

Sergei didn't hesitate. He dodged one final blow from the Keeper and sprinted toward the gate as it opened just wide enough for them to slip through. The Keeper let out a furious roar, but its massive size prevented it from following them through the narrow passage.

As the gate slammed shut behind them, cutting off the Keeper's enraged howls, the group collapsed on the other side, gasping for breath. The sound of the Keeper's blade pounding against the stone gate echoed through the corridor, but for now, they were safe.

Imogen's body shook with adrenaline and fear. "We made it..."

Sergei, breathless and covered in dust, leaned against the wall, his heart still pounding. "Barely."

Eleanor, still clutching her pendant, looked back at the sealed gate, her voice trembling. "That thing... it wasn't just a guardian. It was part of the mansion, wasn't it?"

Sergei nodded grimly. "It was the mansion's last line of defense."

They sat in silence for a moment, the reality of their narrow escape sinking in. The Keeper, monstrous and ancient, had nearly ended them all. But they had survived—at least for now.

"We can't keep doing this," Imogen whispered, her voice heavy with exhaustion. "There's no end to the horrors in this place."

Sergei looked at her, his expression hard but understanding. "We have to keep moving. If we stop, we die."

Imogen nodded, though her heart was heavy with doubt. The mansion was relentless, and each encounter brought them closer to the edge of despair. But they had no choice. The Nightmare Mansion wasn't finished with them yet.

They rose to their feet, the weight of their ordeal pressing down on them as they continued deeper into the nightmare. Behind them, the Keeper's howls echoed through the stone walls, a haunting reminder that the mansion had no intention of letting them go.

Not yet.

Chapter 16: The Blood Moon's Curse

The air inside the Nightmare Mansion had grown thick, oppressive, and choking with a sense of impending doom. The walls themselves seemed to pulse with the dark energy of the Blood Moon, which hung high above the mansion, its crimson glow seeping through every crack and crevice. The light from the moon cast eerie, flickering shadows on the walls, transforming the already sinister atmosphere into something far more malevolent.

Imogen, Sergei, and Eleanor had barely escaped the monstrous Keeper, and though they had found temporary safety behind the sealed gate, the mansion had other plans for them. They could feel it—the energy in the air had shifted. The Blood Moon's influence had grown stronger, and with it, so had the power of the entities that haunted the mansion.

Sergei wiped the sweat from his brow, his breath coming in ragged gasps. "That... thing was bad enough," he muttered, referring to the monstrous guardian they had barely evaded. "Now it feels like the whole place is about to come alive and eat us."

Imogen nodded, her heart pounding in her chest. "It's the Blood Moon. It's getting worse."

Eleanor's hands trembled as she clutched her pendant. "I can feel them. The spirits—they're more aggressive now. They're... feeding off the moon's energy."

Sergei clenched his fists, trying to maintain control. "So we're trapped in a house full of monsters, and the moon's making them stronger? Perfect."

Imogen's eyes flicked to the windows, where the Blood Moon's glow illuminated the twisted architecture of the mansion. "The moon," she whispered, her voice trembling with fear. "It's always been part of this place's power. But now... it's as if the moon is alive."

Suddenly, the temperature in the room dropped, a cold chill sweeping through them like a gust of arctic wind. Shadows swirled at the edges of their vision, moving in unnatural ways, and the walls seemed to stretch and breathe. The faint sound of whispering filled the air, barely audible, like a thousand voices murmuring from the void.

"They're coming," Eleanor whispered, her voice barely above a breath. "The spirits—they're stronger now."

Without warning, the walls began to tremble, and the floor beneath them shifted violently. A loud, bone-chilling wail echoed through the corridors, and from the shadows emerged the first of the supernatural entities.

It was a spectral figure, its form distorted and flickering like a glitch in reality. Its eyes glowed with a deep, fiery red, and its mouth twisted into a grotesque grin. The air around it crackled with dark energy, and as it moved toward them, the temperature plummeted further.

Sergei stepped forward, brandishing his dagger. "Get ready. They're not playing games anymore."

The ghost lunged at them with terrifying speed, its hands outstretched like claws. Sergei dodged to the side, slashing at the entity with his blade, but the weapon passed through its form as though it were made of smoke. The specter shrieked, its voice piercing and maddening.

"We can't fight them!" Imogen shouted, backing away. "They're too strong!"

Eleanor's face was pale as she tried to summon a protective spell, but the entity lashed out, its spectral hand slamming into her chest and knocking her to the ground. She gasped, her body convulsing as the dark energy surged through her.

"Eleanor!" Imogen cried, rushing to her side.

Eleanor's eyes fluttered open, pain etched across her face. "The Blood Moon," she whispered weakly. "It's making them... unstoppable."

Sergei cursed under his breath, his mind racing as more spirits began to materialize around them. They were surrounded—phantoms, wraiths, and other malevolent entities, all empowered by the blood-red light of the moon. The mansion itself seemed to tremble with anticipation, as though it fed off the chaos.

"We have to move!" Sergei shouted, grabbing Imogen by the arm and pulling her away from the approaching spirits. "If we stay here, we're dead."

Imogen helped Eleanor to her feet, though the psychic's movements were slow and pained. "Can you walk?" she asked, her voice filled with concern.

Eleanor nodded weakly, though her face was drawn with exhaustion. "I'll manage."

They ran down the corridor, the spirits pursuing them with unnatural speed. The temperature continued to drop, and the whispers grew louder, filling their minds with dark, twisted thoughts. The influence of the Blood Moon was everywhere, twisting reality, warping their senses.

As they reached the end of the hall, the floor beneath them shifted again, and the walls seemed to close in around them, narrowing the passage. Sergei slammed his shoulder into a door, forcing it open, and the group stumbled into a large, circular chamber.

The room was dominated by a massive stained-glass window that depicted the Blood Moon in all its crimson glory. The light from the moon bathed the chamber in a sickly red glow, and in the center of the room stood a large stone altar, covered in arcane symbols and carvings.

"This must be it," Imogen said, her voice trembling. "The source of the curse."

Sergei stepped forward, his eyes narrowing as he examined the altar. "The mansion's been drawing power from the Blood Moon all along. This altar—it's the key."

Eleanor, still clutching her pendant for protection, nodded weakly. "We need to destroy it. If we break the connection between the mansion and the Blood Moon, we can weaken the entities."

Sergei gritted his teeth, his hand tightening around the hilt of his dagger. "Let's hope it works."

Without hesitation, he raised the dagger and brought it down onto the stone altar. The blade clanged against the surface, sending sparks flying, but the altar remained intact. The room trembled violently, and the light from the Blood Moon seemed to intensify, filling the chamber with an overwhelming sense of dread.

"It's not enough," Imogen said, her voice filled with panic. "The moon's power is too strong."

Suddenly, the ground beneath them cracked open, and from the fissures erupted dark tendrils of energy, reaching out like the grasping hands of the dead. The spirits that had been pursuing them swarmed into the room, their eyes glowing with malevolent fury.

Eleanor collapsed to her knees, her strength failing her as the spirits closed in. "We can't stop it..."

Sergei's eyes locked onto the stained-glass window, where the Blood Moon hung in all its terrible glory. "We need to cut off its light," he said, his voice low and determined.

Imogen's eyes widened. "The window?"

Sergei nodded. "The window. If we can shatter it, we can block the moonlight. It's feeding the mansion's power."

Imogen glanced at Eleanor, who nodded weakly in agreement. "It's our only chance."

Sergei took a deep breath and rushed toward the window, raising his dagger high. The spirits howled, their forms distorting as they surged forward to stop him. But Sergei didn't hesitate. With all the strength he had left, he swung his dagger at the stained glass.

The blade struck the window, and with a deafening crash, the glass shattered. The light from the Blood Moon flickered and dimmed as shards of glass rained down around them. The crimson glow faded, and the room was plunged into darkness.

The spirits let out a collective wail, their forms flickering and distorting as the power that had sustained them began to fade. One by one, the supernatural entities dissolved into nothingness, their connection to the Blood Moon severed.

Imogen fell to her knees, gasping for breath as the oppressive energy in the room began to dissipate. "We did it..."

Sergei lowered his dagger, his body trembling with exhaustion. "For now."

Eleanor, pale and weak, managed a faint smile. "The Blood Moon's curse... it's broken."

But even as the spirits vanished and the Blood Moon's light faded, the mansion remained. Its dark presence still loomed over them, and though they had survived the latest horror, they knew the Nightmare Mansion was far from finished with them.

Not yet.

Chapter 17: Ritual of Despair

The shattering of the stained-glass window had brought them a moment of respite, but as the echoes of broken glass faded, the oppressive weight of the mansion remained. The Blood Moon's influence had been weakened, but the air still thrummed with malevolent energy. It wasn't over. Not yet.

Imogen, Sergei, and Eleanor stood in the aftermath of their latest battle, catching their breath, their hearts pounding with the lingering adrenaline. The room, once bathed in crimson light, now felt eerily quiet, as if the mansion itself was holding its breath.

Imogen wiped the sweat from her brow, her eyes scanning the chamber. "We've broken the moon's hold," she said, though her voice was uncertain. "But the mansion... it's still alive."

Sergei nodded, his expression grim. "That altar didn't just draw power from the Blood Moon. There's something deeper, something older at work here."

Eleanor, still recovering from the psychic onslaught, sat slumped against the wall, her eyes distant. "I can feel it," she whispered, her voice soft but filled with dread. "There's a ritual—an ancient one—woven into the very stones of this place. It's binding the mansion to dark forces."

Sergei glanced at her, his brow furrowing. "A ritual? What kind of ritual?"

Eleanor's hands trembled as she struggled to rise to her feet. "A forbidden one. It explains everything—why the mansion is feeding off the energy of the Blood Moon, why the spirits are bound to this place. The ritual is at the heart of it."

Imogen's eyes widened, realization dawning. "The ritual of despair," she murmured. "I read something about it... long ago. It's ancient magic, the kind no one speaks of anymore."

Sergei frowned. "What does it do?"

Imogen swallowed, her throat dry. "It's a ritual of sacrifice—of despair. The ritual channels the pain, the suffering, and the hopelessness of those within the mansion's walls, turning that energy into power. The mansion becomes a conduit for dark forces, drawing strength from the despair of the living and the dead."

Eleanor nodded weakly. "The mansion has been feeding on us from the moment we entered. Every death, every fear, every moment of despair—it's all part of the ritual."

Sergei's jaw clenched, his hands tightening into fists. "Then how do we stop it?"

Imogen hesitated, her mind racing. The ritual was ancient, forbidden magic—knowledge that had been buried for centuries, perhaps for a good reason. But if they didn't stop it, the mansion would continue its dark cycle, claiming more lives, feeding its insatiable hunger.

"There's only one way," Imogen said slowly. "We have to break the ritual."

Sergei's eyes narrowed. "How?"

Imogen stepped toward the altar, her gaze locked on the strange symbols that still glowed faintly on its surface. "The ritual is bound to this place, to the altar. It was performed here—maybe hundreds of years ago—and it's been feeding on despair ever since. If we can reverse the ritual, we can sever the mansion's connection to the dark forces it's bound to."

Eleanor, still pale but resolute, nodded. "But it won't be easy. The ritual is dangerous. It requires a sacrifice—one that must be given willingly."

Sergei's expression darkened. "What kind of sacrifice?"

Imogen's voice trembled as she spoke. "A life. The ritual was built on despair and death. To break it, someone has to offer themselves willingly. Only then can the cycle be broken."

Silence fell over the group as the weight of Imogen's words sank in. They had come so far, survived so much, only to be faced with an impossible choice.

"There has to be another way," Sergei muttered, shaking his head. "We can't just sacrifice one of us."

Eleanor's eyes were filled with sorrow. "This is the only way. The mansion will keep feeding on us, on anyone who enters, unless the ritual is broken. The blood of the willing is the only thing that can stop it."

Imogen stared at the altar, her heart heavy. The thought of sacrificing one of them—a friend, a comrade—was unbearable. But she knew Eleanor was right. The mansion wouldn't stop until the ritual was undone.

Sergei's voice broke through the silence, his tone hard and resolute. "If that's what it takes to end this, then I'll do it."

Imogen and Eleanor looked at him in shock. "No!" Imogen cried, stepping forward. "You can't—"

"I can," Sergei said firmly, his eyes locking onto hers. "I've lived through enough darkness in my life. I'm not afraid of what comes next. If my death can save you, then it's worth it."

Eleanor shook her head, her voice breaking. "Sergei, no. We can find another way."

Sergei smiled grimly. "You know we can't."

Imogen's eyes filled with tears, her heart breaking. "There has to be another way."

Sergei stepped forward, placing a hand on her shoulder. "You and Eleanor can still make it out of here. This is the only way to stop the mansion, to free the souls trapped here. Let me do this."

Imogen's throat tightened, her tears flowing freely now. "You don't have to die for us..."

Sergei shook his head. "This place has taken enough. I'm not letting it take any more."

Without waiting for their approval, Sergei approached the altar. The air around him seemed to thrum with dark energy, as though the mansion itself was watching, waiting for the ritual to be completed.

Eleanor's voice trembled as she began the incantation to reverse the ritual. The words were ancient, filled with power, and as she spoke, the room began to vibrate, the walls groaning in protest. The altar glowed with an ominous light, the symbols on its surface flaring to life once more.

Sergei knelt before the altar, his face calm, though his eyes were filled with a strange peace. He looked back at Imogen and Eleanor one last time, his expression resolute. "When this is over... get out of here. Live."

Imogen's heart shattered as she watched him. She wanted to scream, to stop the ritual, but she knew it was too late.

Eleanor's voice reached a crescendo, the words of the incantation ringing through the chamber like thunder. The altar pulsed with dark energy, and Sergei closed his eyes, bracing for what was to come.

With a final, guttural word, the ritual was complete.

A blinding light filled the room, and Sergei let out a gasp as the energy of the mansion surged through him. His body convulsed, the dark magic tearing through him, consuming him. And then, in an instant, it was over.

Sergei's lifeless body collapsed to the ground, the ritual complete.

Imogen fell to her knees, sobbing uncontrollably as the mansion's dark power began to unravel. The walls shook, the floors buckled, and the oppressive energy that had filled the air for so long began to fade.

The Ritual of Despair had been broken, but at a terrible cost.

Eleanor knelt beside Imogen, her own tears falling silently as the two of them mourned the loss of their friend. The mansion had claimed another life, but this time, it would be the last.

The Nightmare Mansion's connection to the dark forces had been severed, and as the mansion crumbled around them, Imogen and Eleanor knew they had finally won.

But the victory tasted hollow.

Chapter 18: The Haunting Melody

The mansion was crumbling around them, the walls groaning as the dark forces that had bound it together for centuries unraveled. Imogen and Eleanor had barely survived the Ritual of Despair, but their victory had come at a terrible cost. Sergei's sacrifice weighed heavily on them both, his final words echoing in their minds. They were so close to escape, yet the mansion still held one final horror.

Imogen wiped away her tears, her heart heavy with grief, but there was no time to stop. The mansion was collapsing, and they needed to leave before they were buried with it. Eleanor, pale and weak from the psychic strain, leaned against the wall, struggling to catch her breath.

"We need to move," Imogen said, her voice strained. "We can mourn him later. If we stay here, we'll die too."

Eleanor nodded, though her eyes were distant. The horrors of the mansion had taken their toll on her, and each step felt like a battle. But she knew Imogen was right—they couldn't afford to stop now.

As they moved deeper through the twisting corridors, the oppressive silence was shattered by a soft, melodic sound. At first, it was barely audible—a faint, eerie tune carried on the cold wind that blew through the cracked walls. It was haunting, beautiful in a way that made the hair on the back of Imogen's neck stand on end.

"Do you hear that?" Imogen asked, her voice low.

Eleanor paused, listening. "Yes," she whispered. "It sounds like... music."

The melody was soft and lilting, almost hypnotic, and as it grew louder, its beauty became more unsettling. The notes seemed to twist in the air, haunting and dissonant, as though they were not meant for human ears. Imogen's heart quickened, her instincts screaming that this was not something they should follow, but Eleanor seemed captivated.

"It's beautiful," Eleanor murmured, her eyes wide as she took a step toward the source of the sound.

Imogen grabbed her arm, pulling her back. "Eleanor, no. It's a trick. It has to be."

But Eleanor's face was transfixed, her eyes glazed over as if in a trance. "It's calling me..."

Imogen's grip tightened, her voice shaking. "We can't—Eleanor, snap out of it!"

The melody grew louder, more intense, and with it came a rising sense of dread. Imogen could feel it—something was wrong, horribly wrong. The music wasn't just sound; it was something more, something alive. It wrapped itself around them, pulling them deeper into its spell.

"Eleanor, please!" Imogen shouted, trying to shake her friend from the trance. But Eleanor's gaze was fixed on the distant shadows, where the melody seemed to be coming from.

"I have to find it," Eleanor whispered, her voice distant. "I have to follow it..."

Before Imogen could stop her, Eleanor broke free from her grasp and began walking toward the source of the melody, her steps slow and deliberate, as though she were sleepwalking.

"No!" Imogen cried, running after her. "Eleanor, don't! It's a trap!"

But Eleanor didn't respond. Her eyes were glazed, her face blank as she followed the haunting tune. Imogen's heart pounded in her chest as she reached for Eleanor again, but the music seemed to warp around them, distorting reality itself. The walls of the mansion shifted, elongating and twisting, pulling Eleanor farther away.

"Eleanor!" Imogen screamed, her voice echoing through the shifting hallways.

But Eleanor was too far gone. The melody grew louder, more aggressive, and with it, Eleanor's movements became more erratic. She clutched her head, wincing as if in pain, but still, she pressed forward, her steps unsteady. The music seemed to pierce through her mind, twisting her thoughts, turning her own memories and fears against her.

Imogen watched in horror as Eleanor began to mutter to herself, her voice frantic. "It's in my head... I can't stop it... It won't stop..."

Suddenly, Eleanor let out a scream of pure terror, her hands clawing at her own face as if trying to tear the sound out of her mind. Blood trickled from her ears, her eyes wide with madness as the melody continued to worm its way into her thoughts, driving her to the edge of insanity.

"Eleanor, stop!" Imogen cried, rushing toward her.

But Eleanor was beyond saving. Her body convulsed violently, and with a guttural scream, she threw herself against the wall, slamming her head into the stone with a sickening thud. Blood splattered across the floor as Eleanor collapsed, her body twitching, her mind shattered by the relentless, haunting melody.

Imogen fell to her knees beside her, tears streaming down her face. "Eleanor, no..."

But Eleanor's lifeless eyes stared up at the ceiling, her face twisted in agony. The melody continued to play, soft and lilting, a grotesque mockery of the beauty it once held.

Imogen sobbed, clutching her friend's body as the music finally began to fade, leaving behind only silence and the crushing weight of loss. The mansion had claimed yet another soul, feeding on Eleanor's despair, her fear, her madness.

For a long moment, Imogen knelt there, her body shaking with grief. She had lost everything—Sergei, Stanley, Samantha... and now Eleanor. The mansion had taken them all, and now it was coming for her.

But as Imogen stood, her heart hardened with resolve. The mansion might have taken her friends, but it would not take her. She would survive. She had to.

Wiping away her tears, Imogen turned away from Eleanor's body and began to move forward, the weight of her grief fueling her determination. The Nightmare Mansion still pulsed with dark energy, but Imogen would not let it claim her. Not yet.

The haunting melody still lingered in the air, a faint echo of the madness it had unleashed, but Imogen pressed on. She was the last one standing, and she would not fall. Not without a fight.

The mansion had taken so much, but Imogen was still alive. And she would find a way out.

Chapter 19: The Forest of Shadows

Imogen stood at the edge of the mansion's annexed forest, her heart pounding in her chest. The mansion had been a maze of horrors, but now, standing before the dense wall of twisted trees, she felt a new kind of fear. The forest loomed before her, its canopy so thick that it blocked out the sky entirely, casting everything in an oppressive darkness. The air smelled of damp earth and decay, and the trees themselves seemed to pulse with malevolent energy.

Eleanor's body, now left behind, haunted Imogen's thoughts, but there was no time to grieve. The mansion had pushed her toward this forest as if guiding her to face whatever waited in its depths. Imogen swallowed hard, the weight of her losses pressing down on her. She had no choice but to move forward.

"Stay sharp," Imogen muttered to herself, her voice a shaky reminder to stay vigilant.

The trees closed in around her as she ventured deeper, their gnarled branches reaching out like twisted claws. Every step felt like a journey into the unknown, each rustle of leaves or snap of a twig sending a jolt of fear through her. The further she went, the darker it became, until even the faintest light from the Blood Moon no longer pierced the canopy.

And then, the sounds began—whispers, faint and distant, as if the forest itself was alive, watching her.

Imogen paused, her breath catching in her throat. The whispering seemed to come from all directions, low and unintelligible. She gripped the dagger she had taken from Sergei's body tighter, her knuckles white.

"Show yourself," she whispered into the darkness, though she knew she didn't want to see whatever was lurking there.

A soft rustling echoed from the shadows, followed by the unmistakable sound of something moving quickly just out of sight. Imogen's heart raced as she spun around, trying to catch a glimpse of whatever was stalking her. But the forest was too dark, too thick. The trees swayed unnaturally in the windless air, and the shadows seemed to move of their own accord.

Then, from the corner of her eye, she saw it—a figure, barely more than a silhouette, slipping between the trees. It was humanoid, but its body was elongated, unnaturally thin, with limbs that stretched too far, its form blending into the shadows.

Imogen took a step back, her breath shallow. "What... what are you?"

The figure didn't answer, but as it moved closer, more figures began to emerge from the darkness. Dozens of them, all shifting and swaying like wraiths, their forms blending seamlessly into the shadows. Their eyes glowed faintly, watching her with a predatory hunger.

Imogen's blood ran cold. Shadow creatures. She had heard stories of them—beings that lived in the darkness, feeding on fear and despair. They were relentless hunters, drawn to places of suffering, and the forest had become their domain.

She turned to run, but before she could take more than a few steps, the creatures surged forward, their movements unnaturally fast. Imogen's heart pounded in her ears as she sprinted through the forest, her feet stumbling over roots and rocks hidden beneath the thick undergrowth.

The shadow creatures gave chase, their forms darting between the trees with terrifying speed. Imogen could hear them behind her, the soft rustling of leaves, the low, hungry growls that sent chills down her spine.

As she ran, the forest seemed to twist and change around her, the path she had taken moments before now unrecognizable. The trees grew closer, their branches reaching out to block her path. The ground beneath her feet shifted, pulling her deeper into the dark heart of the forest.

A shadow creature lunged at her from the side, its clawed hand swiping through the air just inches from her face. Imogen stumbled, barely managing to dodge the attack. She raised Sergei's dagger, slashing wildly at the creature, but the blade passed through it as though it were made of mist.

Panic surged through her. "I can't fight them," she gasped, her voice filled with fear. "They're made of darkness."

The creatures closed in, their glowing eyes fixed on her as they moved in for the kill. Imogen's mind raced, trying to find a way out, but the forest was a maze, and the shadows seemed to shift and move with the creatures, trapping her at every turn.

One of the shadow creatures lunged forward, its claws raking across her arm. Imogen cried out in pain as blood welled up from the gashes, her vision blurring with the sudden agony. She stumbled backward, clutching her arm, but the creatures showed no mercy. They pressed forward, their movements growing more frenzied, their eyes glowing brighter as they fed on her fear.

Imogen's legs gave out, and she fell to her knees, her breath coming in ragged gasps. The creatures circled her now, their whispers filling her mind, their claws poised to strike. She knew this was the end.

But then, from the depths of her despair, something shifted.

The pendant Eleanor had given her—the protective charm she had clung to for so long—began to glow softly at her chest. Imogen's eyes widened as a faint warmth spread through her body, pushing back the cold grip of the shadow creatures. The creatures recoiled, their forms flickering as the light from the pendant grew stronger.

Imogen's heart raced with a renewed sense of hope. The pendant—it was protecting her.

She gripped the pendant tightly, its warmth giving her the strength to rise to her feet. The shadow creatures hissed in anger, their movements growing more erratic as they tried to close in on her, but the light from the pendant was too strong. It pushed them back, forcing them to retreat into the shadows.

Imogen stood tall, her heart pounding with adrenaline. The creatures circled her still, watching from the darkness, but they couldn't touch her now. The pendant glowed brighter, casting a protective barrier around her as she moved through the forest.

For the first time since entering the Nightmare Mansion, Imogen felt a glimmer of hope. She had lost so much—Sergei, Eleanor, Stanley—but she was still alive. And as long as she had this light, the shadows couldn't claim her.

The creatures watched from the darkness, their glowing eyes filled with hunger and frustration. But they couldn't follow her. Not anymore.

With renewed determination, Imogen pressed on, leaving the Forest of Shadows behind as she ventured deeper into the unknown. The mansion had thrown every horror it could at her, but she was still standing. And now, more than ever, she was determined to survive.

The Nightmare Mansion wasn't finished with her yet, but neither was she.

Chapter 20: The Cavern's Depths

Imogen emerged from the twisted forest, battered but alive, her pendant still glowing faintly at her chest. The eerie forest had nearly claimed her, but with the shadow creatures held at bay, she had managed to escape their clutches. Her path led her deeper into the heart of the Nightmare Mansion's grounds, where the land sloped downward into a dark and foreboding cavern.

The entrance to the cavern yawned before her like the mouth of some great beast, its jagged rocks and dark passageways promising more horrors. But Imogen had no choice. She was alone now, the last survivor, and every step she took brought her closer to the answers she desperately sought. Answers about the mansion, about its connection to the Blood Moon, and the forces that had claimed the lives of her friends.

With a deep breath, she stepped into the cavern.

The air inside was cool and damp, the walls slick with moisture. Imogen could hear the faint sound of water dripping somewhere in the distance, a rhythmic, almost soothing contrast to the chaos she had endured. But there was something else, too—an undercurrent of energy that hummed through the very stone of the cavern, like a heartbeat deep within the earth.

She descended further, her footsteps echoing off the walls, the light from her pendant casting faint shadows around her. The path wound downward, twisting and turning through the rock until it opened up into a vast chamber.

Imogen's breath caught in her throat as she stepped into the room. The cavern was immense, its ceiling rising far above her, lost in the darkness. The walls were lined with strange symbols and carvings, much like those she had seen throughout the mansion. But here, in the cavern's depths, they were older, more intricate—clearly the work of a long-forgotten civilization.

In the center of the chamber stood several stone pedestals, each holding an artifact. Imogen approached cautiously, her eyes scanning the room for any sign of danger. The air was thick with the weight of history, as though the very stones held memories of the past.

She stopped before the first pedestal, her heart racing as she examined the artifact resting upon it. It was a small, intricately carved tablet made of a dark stone that seemed to absorb the light around it. The symbols etched into its surface were unlike anything Imogen had seen before, but there was something about them—something familiar.

She reached out, her fingers brushing against the cool surface of the tablet. As soon as she touched it, a surge of energy coursed through her, and for a brief moment, her mind was flooded with visions—flashes of rituals, of blood and fire, of ancient figures gathered in the darkness, performing acts of unspeakable power.

Imogen gasped, pulling her hand away. Her heart pounded in her chest, and she stumbled back, her mind reeling from what she had seen.

"This is it," she whispered to herself, her voice trembling. "This is the key. The mansion's origins."

She moved to the next pedestal, where another artifact rested—a strange, twisted piece of metal shaped like a ring, its surface covered in the same ancient symbols. Imogen studied it for a moment before picking it up. The moment her fingers closed around it, the visions returned—this time more vivid, more intense.

She saw a great gathering of figures cloaked in shadow, standing at the edge of a blood-red sea, the Blood Moon hanging high above them. They were chanting, their voices low and rhythmic, their hands raised toward the sky as they performed a ritual. At the center of the gathering stood a great stone structure—an altar, much like the one she had seen in the mansion. And from it, dark energy flowed, feeding the mansion's malevolence.

Imogen's grip tightened on the ring as the vision faded. The cavern felt suddenly colder, the air more oppressive. She knew now—this was where it had all begun. The mansion, the Blood Moon, the ritual of despair—it was all tied to this ancient civilization, these artifacts.

The mansion was a vessel for something far older than she had realized. Its origins were rooted in these forgotten rituals, and its power came from the dark forces they had awakened. Imogen's mind raced, trying to piece it all together.

"They created the mansion," she whispered, her voice barely audible. "It's not just haunted. It was built as a conduit, a way to channel the Blood Moon's power."

As she placed the ring back on the pedestal, her attention was drawn to a large mural on the far wall. It depicted a figure standing before the mansion, their arms outstretched as dark tendrils of energy flowed from the Blood Moon above and into the building. Around the figure were symbols—symbols of sacrifice, of blood, of death.

Imogen's stomach twisted as she realized what the mural was telling her. The mansion had been designed not just as a conduit, but as a prison for the dark forces summoned during the ritual. The spirits, the shadow creatures, the malevolent energy—it had all been contained within the mansion's walls, feeding off the despair of those who entered, growing stronger with each death.

And now, with the Blood Moon in its full power, the mansion was no longer content to remain a prison. It was expanding, its influence spreading beyond its walls, seeking more souls to consume.

Imogen's heart sank. She had thought breaking the Blood Moon's connection would be enough to weaken the mansion, but now she saw the truth. The mansion's power was older than the moon itself. It was tied to something much darker—something that had been growing for centuries, waiting for the right moment to break free.

Suddenly, a low rumble echoed through the cavern, shaking the ground beneath her feet. Imogen stumbled, her eyes darting around the chamber. The symbols on the walls began to glow faintly, pulsing with the same dark energy she had felt in the mansion.

She had to leave. Now.

Grabbing the tablet from the pedestal, Imogen turned and ran toward the exit. The cavern shook violently as she raced through the twisting tunnels, the symbols on the walls glowing brighter, the air growing thick with energy. The mansion was awakening, and it wouldn't let her leave without a fight.

As she neared the entrance to the cavern, the shadows around her began to shift, coalescing into the familiar forms of the shadow creatures. They moved faster now, more aggressive, their glowing eyes locked onto her as they closed in.

Imogen's breath came in ragged gasps as she sprinted through the darkness, her mind racing. She clutched the tablet tightly to her chest, knowing that it held the key to stopping the mansion once and for all.

But would she survive long enough to use it?

With the shadow creatures closing in, Imogen pushed herself harder, her legs burning with the effort. The exit to the cavern loomed ahead, and beyond it, the twisted halls of the Nightmare Mansion awaited her.

The final battle was coming, and Imogen knew she had little time left.

As she escaped the caverns and entered the mansion once more, the tablet pulsed with a dark, ancient power, and Imogen knew that the true fight had only just begun.

Chapter 21: The Hall of Faces

Imogen stumbled back into the mansion, her breath ragged and her heart racing. The air was thicker now, heavy with a sense of impending doom. The weight of the ancient tablet she clutched in her hands felt overwhelming, as though it carried centuries of pain and suffering within its cold surface. She had barely escaped the caverns, her mind still reeling from the revelations about the mansion's true purpose.

As she moved through the twisted corridors, each step echoed with a sense of finality. Imogen knew she was running out of time. The mansion was stirring, its dark heart coming alive, and the Blood Moon's curse was still pressing down on everything around her. There was something else waiting for her—something the mansion had planned as its final torment.

She found herself drawn to a long, narrow hallway, the walls lined with strange, dimly lit sconces. The air was cold, and an eerie silence filled the space. Imogen paused at the entrance, a deep sense of dread washing over her. She didn't want to go in, but something pulled her forward—an irresistible force she couldn't explain.

The hall stretched endlessly before her, and as she took her first tentative steps, the sconces flickered, casting long, shifting shadows across the walls. Imogen's breath caught in her throat as she saw them.

Faces. Dozens—no, hundreds—of faces.

The walls were covered in them, their features twisted in expressions of fear, agony, and despair. Each face was unique, yet they all shared the same haunted, hopeless look, as if frozen in the moment of their death. They stared down at her with hollow, empty eyes, their mouths twisted into silent screams.

Imogen's pulse quickened as she recognized them. They were the mansion's victims—the people who had been lured into this cursed place over the centuries, only to be consumed by its darkness.

"No..." she whispered, shaking her head in disbelief. "This can't be real."

But the faces were real. They watched her with unblinking eyes, their expressions mocking her, taunting her with the fate that awaited her. She could feel their despair, their pain, as though it was seeping from the walls and into her very soul.

As she moved further down the hall, the faces seemed to grow more animated. Their eyes followed her, their expressions shifting subtly. Some of them grinned, their lips curling into grotesque smiles, while others wept silently, their tears turning into blood that dripped down the walls.

Suddenly, a voice echoed through the hall—low, whispering, like the sound of a thousand voices speaking at once.

"Imogen..."

She froze, her heart pounding in her chest. The voice was unmistakable—it was Eleanor's.

"Imogen, why didn't you save me?" the voice whispered, filled with anguish. "Why did you leave me to die?"

Imogen's breath came in short, shallow gasps as she turned toward one of the faces on the wall. There, among the countless others, was Eleanor's face, twisted in an expression of sorrow and betrayal.

"No," Imogen whispered, her eyes filling with tears. "That's not you... you're gone..."

But Eleanor's face remained, her eyes locked onto Imogen's. "You let me die," the voice accused. "You watched as the mansion took me, and you did nothing."

Imogen staggered backward, shaking her head. "I tried to save you! I did everything I could!"

The faces around her began to move, their expressions warping into twisted versions of the people she had known—Sergei, Stanley, Samantha. They all stared at her, their faces filled with accusations, their voices joining Eleanor's in a chorus of torment.

"You could have saved us, Imogen," Sergei's voice growled, his face contorted in anger. "But you didn't. You ran. You left us to die."

Stanley's face appeared next, his hollow eyes staring at her. "You were too afraid. Too weak."

Imogen's vision blurred with tears as the voices grew louder, more insistent. They surrounded her, echoing through her mind, drowning out her thoughts.

"Stop!" she cried, covering her ears. "Please, stop!"

But the voices didn't stop. The faces continued to shift, showing her the faces of the dead—the people she had known, the strangers who had come before her, all of them victims of the mansion's insatiable hunger.

"Your fate is sealed," the voices hissed. "You cannot escape. You are one of us now."

Imogen fell to her knees, her body trembling with fear and grief. The faces were right. No one who had entered the Nightmare Mansion had ever escaped. They were all here, trapped forever in the walls of the cursed building, their souls consumed by the darkness that lurked within.

But as the despair threatened to consume her, something flickered inside her. A spark of defiance, of hope. Imogen wasn't like the others. She had come farther than anyone before her. She had discovered the mansion's secrets, unraveled its dark history. And she had the tablet—the key to stopping it all.

She forced herself to stand, her legs shaking but her resolve hardening. The voices continued to taunt her, but she ignored them, focusing on the tablet in her hands. The ancient artifact hummed with energy, and she could feel its power coursing through her.

"You're wrong," she whispered, her voice trembling but filled with determination. "I won't end up like you."

The faces on the walls contorted in anger, their expressions growing more grotesque. The whispers turned into screams, filling the hallway with deafening sound, but Imogen held her ground.

With a surge of energy, she raised the tablet, its dark surface glowing with a faint light. She could feel the connection between the tablet and the mansion—the ancient ritual that had bound it to the darkness. And she knew what she had to do.

Taking a deep breath, she channeled all her willpower into the tablet, focusing on the symbols she had seen in the caverns. The symbols glowed brighter, and the energy within the tablet surged, filling the hall with a blinding light.

The faces on the walls screamed in agony as the light washed over them, their twisted forms melting away into the darkness. The walls trembled, and the voices grew fainter, until at last, the hall was silent once more.

Imogen stood alone, the tablet still glowing in her hands. The faces were gone, and the oppressive weight of the mansion's curse seemed to lift, if only for a moment.

She had won this battle, but the war was far from over.

With renewed determination, Imogen turned and continued down the hallway, the tablet's power still thrumming in her hands. The mansion had thrown everything it had at her—its horrors, its tricks—but she was still standing.

And now, more than ever, she was determined to see it fall.

Chapter 22: The Final Stand

Imogen pressed on through the mansion, her footsteps echoing in the vast emptiness. The Hall of Faces had nearly broken her spirit, but the light from the ancient tablet she carried gave her the strength to continue. The mansion still pulsed with malevolent energy, and the air was thick with tension, as if the building itself knew the endgame was near. She could feel it—something was coming, something terrible.

The corridors twisted and turned, leading her deeper into the heart of the mansion. With every step, the walls seemed to close in, the shadows growing darker, more oppressive. She had survived horrors beyond comprehension, but now, at the edge of despair, she knew this was the final test. Whatever the mansion had left, it would throw at her now.

Suddenly, the air shifted—a chilling wind swept through the halls, bringing with it the unmistakable scent of decay. Imogen's breath caught in her throat as the shadows around her began to writhe and move, forming shapes that slithered along the walls and ceiling.

A low growl echoed through the air, and from the darkness, the monstrous forms of the mansion's horrors began to emerge. They were a grotesque amalgamation of all the creatures she had faced—shadow creatures with glowing eyes, twisted spirits that had haunted the halls, and even the grotesque figure of the Labyrinth's Keeper. But this time, they were more powerful, more real, as if the mansion had drawn them from the deepest parts of its malevolent heart.

Imogen gripped the tablet tightly, her heart racing. She was alone now—no Sergei, no Eleanor, no one to help her fight. The mansion had claimed them all. And yet, as the creatures closed in around her, she steeled herself for what was to come.

"This is it," she whispered to herself. "The final battle."

The creatures surged forward, their forms twisting and shifting, their eyes burning with malice. Imogen raised the tablet, its surface glowing brighter as the ancient symbols activated. She could feel the power within it, the same energy that had once been used to bind the mansion to the dark forces. But the tablet was a double-edged sword—it could either destroy the mansion or unleash its horrors in full.

She had to make a choice.

The first creature lunged at her, a mass of shadows and teeth, but Imogen was ready. She swung the tablet, and a pulse of energy shot from its surface, slamming into the creature and sending it flying backward. The impact shook the air, but more creatures followed, their grotesque forms relentless as they charged toward her.

Imogen gritted her teeth, focusing all her strength into the tablet. Another pulse of energy erupted from it, blasting the creatures back, but it was like fighting an endless tide. For every monster she pushed away, another two took its place.

"Come on!" she screamed, her voice echoing through the halls. "Is that all you've got?"

But the mansion wasn't finished yet. The air grew colder, and from the shadows emerged something far worse than the creatures she had been battling. It was a figure—tall, cloaked in darkness, with glowing red eyes that burned with an ancient, unfathomable hatred. Its presence was suffocating, and the very ground trembled as it approached.

Imogen's heart sank. This was the true face of the mansion, the embodiment of the darkness that had consumed it for centuries. The tablet in her hands trembled, the symbols flickering as if even its ancient power wasn't enough to stand against this force.

"You will not leave," the figure whispered, its voice like a thousand tortured souls speaking as one. "You are mine."

Imogen took a step back, her hands trembling. She had fought so hard, lost so much, but now, standing before the source of the mansion's power, she felt small, insignificant. How could she fight something this powerful?

The figure raised its hand, and the shadows around it twisted and coiled, forming tendrils that reached out toward her. Imogen raised the tablet again, but this time, the energy it emitted was weaker, flickering as the dark power of the mansion pressed down on it.

"No," she whispered, her voice cracking. "I won't let you win."

But even as she spoke, she could feel the weight of the mansion's power crushing down on her. The creatures circled her, their glowing eyes watching, waiting for the moment when she would fall. The figure loomed closer, its red eyes burning with malevolent glee.

Imogen fell to her knees, her strength failing. The tablet slipped from her hands, clattering to the ground as the darkness closed in around her.

"You are too late," the figure hissed. "You cannot stop what has already been set in motion."

The shadows pressed in, suffocating her, draining the last of her hope. Imogen gasped for breath, her vision blurring as the darkness consumed her.

But then, in the depths of her despair, a voice echoed in her mind—Sergei's voice, calm and steady.

"You're stronger than you think, Imogen."

Her eyes snapped open, and with a surge of determination, she reached for the tablet. The ancient symbols flared to life, brighter than ever before, and Imogen pushed herself to her feet.

"I'm not done yet," she growled, her voice filled with defiance.

The figure recoiled, its eyes narrowing as the tablet's light grew stronger. Imogen raised it high, channeling every last ounce of energy she had into the ancient artifact. The light from the tablet exploded outward, engulfing the creatures, the shadows, and the figure itself.

The mansion trembled violently, its walls cracking, its very foundation shaking as the power of the tablet clashed with the darkness that had consumed it. The figure let out a deafening roar as the light tore through it, and for a moment, it seemed as though Imogen had won.

But then, the light faltered.

The tablet, drained of its power, flickered one last time and then went dark. The shadows surged forward once more, and Imogen's heart sank as she realized that her efforts had been in vain.

The mansion's horrors pressed in around her, their eyes filled with hunger, and Imogen knew that this was the end. She had fought with everything she had, but the mansion was too strong, too ancient, its evil too deeply rooted to be undone.

As the darkness closed in, Imogen whispered a final, broken plea.

"I'm sorry."

And then, with a final surge, the shadows consumed her, and the Nightmare Mansion claimed its last victim.

The halls fell silent once more, the echoes of the final stand fading into the void. The mansion stood as it always had, its hunger sated for now, waiting for the next souls foolish enough to enter its cursed walls.

And high above, the Blood Moon continued to shine.

Chapter 23: The Last Breath

The mansion was eerily quiet, a stillness settling over its darkened halls. The air, once charged with tension and the sounds of battle, had grown thick and oppressive. Imogen lay in the heart of the Nightmare Mansion, her body broken, her spirit shattered. The darkness, relentless and unforgiving, had consumed her, leaving her as little more than a vessel for the ancient evil that pulsed through the mansion's walls.

The final light from the tablet had long since faded, its power drained, unable to stop the dark forces that had been set in motion centuries ago. Imogen's breaths were shallow, each one more labored than the last as she lay on the cold stone floor, her eyes barely open, staring into the abyss. She had fought with every ounce of strength she had, but in the end, the mansion had claimed her like all the others before her.

Above her, the Blood Moon cast its crimson glow through the cracks in the ceiling, its light feeding the malevolent energy that swirled through the mansion. The shadows around her seemed to pulse in time with her slowing heartbeat, drawn to her final moments of life, ready to consume what little remained of her soul.

Imogen's vision blurred, her mind swimming in and out of consciousness. She could hear faint whispers in the darkness, voices that seemed to come from everywhere and nowhere, mocking her, taunting her for daring to think she could defeat the mansion.

"Foolish... so foolish..."

She tried to move, but her body was too weak. The energy had been drained from her long ago, and now she was nothing more than a shell, waiting for the inevitable end. Her thoughts drifted to her friends—Sergei, Eleanor, Stanley, Samantha—each of them had fallen to the horrors of this place, each life fueling the mansion's insatiable hunger.

And now it was her turn.

"Did you really think you could escape?" a voice whispered in her ear, its tone filled with cruel amusement. "You were always destined to die here."

Imogen's heart raced, a flicker of defiance igniting in her chest, but it was quickly snuffed out by the overwhelming despair that flooded her mind. The voices grew louder, more insistent, pressing in on her from all sides.

"There is no escape... only the darkness."

Her breaths came in shallow gasps, her body convulsing as the shadows pressed in closer, their cold, spectral hands reaching for her. Imogen could feel her soul slipping away, being torn from her body by the very forces she had fought so hard to resist.

But even as the darkness closed in, a single tear slipped from her eye, tracing a path down her bloodied cheek. It was the last trace of her humanity, the last flicker of light before she was swallowed by the void.

The shadows surged forward, enveloping her completely, and with a final, ragged breath, Imogen's body went still. The darkness that had consumed the mansion for centuries surged through her, feasting on her despair, her fear, her last breath. Her death wasn't just the end—it was fuel for the mansion's dark heart, empowering the evil that had been festering within its walls for centuries.

The energy in the air shifted, growing stronger, more potent. The shadows that had once flickered in the corners of the mansion now pulsed with a newfound vitality, their forms more solid, more aggressive. The spirits that haunted the halls grew stronger, their malevolent presence palpable. The mansion itself seemed to groan in satisfaction, its walls reverberating with the power it had gained from Imogen's death.

From the ceiling above, the Blood Moon shone brighter than ever, its red light spilling through the cracks and bathing the mansion in an ominous glow. The moon had been waiting for this moment, for the mansion to consume the last of the souls that had dared to challenge it. Now, with Imogen's death, the ritual was complete. The dark forces bound to the mansion had been fed, and their power surged, filling the building with an overwhelming sense of dread.

The whispers in the darkness grew louder, no longer taunting but triumphant.

"We have won."

The mansion, once a cursed prison for the dark forces that had been bound to it, had become something far more dangerous. It was no longer content to feed on the occasional lost soul that wandered into its halls. Now, it sought more. The Blood Moon's influence was spreading, and soon the mansion's reach would extend beyond its walls, claiming more lives, feeding on more despair.

Imogen's lifeless body lay on the floor, her face twisted in a final expression of pain and fear. She had fought to the bitter end, but in the end, she had been no match for the darkness that had taken root in the mansion long ago.

The mansion's hunger had been sated, but only for a moment. Soon, it would hunger again. It always did.

As the last flicker of life drained from Imogen's body, the shadows around her pulsed with dark energy, empowered by her death. The mansion itself seemed to take a breath, its walls trembling as if alive. And then, in the silence that followed, the mansion waited.

The Nightmare Mansion was eternal, and its hunger would never be satisfied.

High above, the Blood Moon continued to shine, its light growing ever stronger, ever redder.

And somewhere in the distance, the sound of footsteps echoed through the halls.

The mansion was ready for its next victims.

The darkness would never end.

Chapter 24: The Mansion's Awakening

The Nightmare Mansion had fallen into an unnatural silence. Imogen's final breath had been taken, and the dark forces within the mansion surged with newfound strength. The air crackled with energy, thick and suffocating, as if the very walls of the mansion were alive, pulsing with malevolence. The Blood Moon above bathed the landscape in its deep red glow, casting eerie shadows across the twisted corridors and halls.

The mansion groaned, as though it was awakening from a long, restless slumber. Every death within its walls had fed its insatiable hunger, each soul consumed fueling its dark power. Now, with Imogen's passing, the mansion had crossed a threshold. It no longer needed to wait for its prey to wander in. It had grown too strong, its influence too far-reaching. The boundaries that had once kept the evil contained within its walls were dissolving.

Imogen's body lay still, her lifeless eyes staring up at the cracked ceiling. Around her, the shadows writhed, pulsing with energy, feeding off the remnants of her despair. Her death was the final key, and with it, the mansion's transformation was complete.

A low rumble shook the foundations of the mansion, dust falling from the ceiling as the walls trembled. The carvings and symbols that had been etched into the stone for centuries began to glow with a deep crimson light, their ancient power reawakening. The air around the mansion vibrated with the hum of dark magic, and the ground outside trembled as the mansion's reach began to extend beyond its cursed walls.

In the nearby town of Ravenswood, the streets lay quiet, oblivious to the terror that was spreading from the mansion. But deep within the town, something had shifted. The influence of the Nightmare Mansion seeped through the earth like a dark fog, creeping into every corner, every shadow. The townspeople, unaware of the looming danger, continued with their lives, but soon, they would feel it—the creeping dread that came with the mansion's awakening.

Within the mansion, the halls began to change. The corridors stretched and twisted, their dimensions warping, defying logic and physics. The rooms expanded and contracted, shifting in ways that made no sense. The very architecture of the mansion was alive, its dark heart pulsing with a hunger that could never be satisfied. The faces of the souls trapped within the walls contorted in agony, their mouths frozen in silent screams, their eyes following every movement as if they, too, were aware of the mansion's growing power.

Then came the whispers.

They echoed through the halls, soft at first, but growing louder with each passing moment. The voices of the dead, of those who had been consumed by the mansion, filled the air with their endless chorus of despair.

"Join us..."

"You cannot escape..."

"We are forever..."

The mansion was no longer simply a haunted building; it had become a living, breathing entity, sustained by the despair and death of those who had entered its walls. The Blood Moon's influence had corrupted the very essence of the mansion, turning it into a conduit for dark forces older than time itself. And now, it sought more—more lives, more souls, more fear.

From the shadows, the creatures that had once hunted the survivors began to emerge, their forms shifting and twisting. They were stronger now, more real, their eyes burning with a hunger that mirrored the mansion's own. The shadow creatures, the wraiths, the monstrous guardians—they were all part of the mansion's dark web, extensions of its will.

In the heart of the mansion, deep within its hidden chambers, the altar that had once been the center of the Ritual of Despair glowed with a fierce, malevolent light. The symbols carved into its surface pulsed with power, the energy of the Blood Moon flowing through them like a river of darkness. The altar had become a focal point for the mansion's growing strength, its connection to the ancient forces that had been awakened.

Suddenly, the mansion let out a deep, guttural groan, and the very ground beneath it seemed to pulse in response. The fog that had spread from the mansion's grounds began to thicken, crawling toward Ravenswood with unstoppable intent. The town, blissfully unaware of the horrors that lay on the horizon, would soon be consumed, just as the mansion had consumed so many before it.

But this time, it would be different.

This time, the mansion's hunger was no longer limited to those who dared to enter its walls. Its reach was growing, its influence spreading beyond the boundaries of its cursed grounds. The Blood Moon had given it the power to extend its grip, and soon, no one would be safe.

In the mansion's central chamber, a large mirror hung on the wall—cracked and smeared with dust, its surface warped. But as the mansion awakened, the mirror began to glow, the cracks filling with a dark, shimmering light. Reflected within its surface were not the rooms of the mansion, but the faces of those who would soon fall victim to its curse.

The mirror showed the future.

The faces of the townspeople, their eyes wide with terror, their mouths open in silent screams, flickered in and out of the reflection. They had no idea what was coming for them, no idea that their fate had already been sealed by the dark forces that now controlled the Nightmare Mansion.

The fog reached the edge of Ravenswood, its dark tendrils creeping into the streets, winding through the alleys and slipping beneath doors. Those who slept in their beds stirred, their dreams turning to nightmares as the mansion's influence seeped into their minds. The once peaceful town would soon become a battleground, its people unaware that they were already trapped in a fight for their souls.

Back in the mansion, the altar's glow intensified, casting long shadows across the room. The whispers grew louder, their chorus rising to a fever pitch.

"We are eternal..."

"We are unstoppable..."

"We are coming..."

The Nightmare Mansion had awakened fully now, and with each soul it claimed, it would only grow stronger. Its reach would extend further, its hunger would never be satisfied, and the Blood Moon would continue to shine, casting its crimson light over a world that would soon fall under the mansion's curse.

The town of Ravenswood, the first to fall, would only be the beginning.

And as the mansion pulsed with dark energy, the whispers of the dead echoed through its halls, a chilling promise of what was to come.

"Welcome to eternity."

Epilogue: Infernal Revelations

In the aftermath of the Blood Moon's chilling glow, the world shifted. The once quiet town of Ravenswood had become a focal point for something far beyond the comprehension of its citizens. As the dark fog that had enveloped the town spread, panic gripped the world. Reports of strange occurrences, people disappearing, and haunting nightmares sweeping through entire regions forced international leaders to confront the unthinkable.

The United Nations Security Council convened in an emergency session. The room buzzed with tension as representatives from major nations sat at the round table, their faces pale and anxious. Satellite images of Ravenswood—now a dark blot on the map, obscured by a thick, impenetrable fog—were projected onto large screens behind them. Footage from nearby towns showed strange, unnatural phenomena: lights flickering in patterns that defied logic, strange shapes moving through the mist, and people wandering aimlessly with blank, haunted expressions.

Ambassador Elena Vargas, representing the United States, leaned forward, her eyes scanning the room. "We can no longer ignore this. Ravenswood is just the beginning. This... infection—whatever it is—is spreading. We've had reports of similar events in neighboring towns, and it won't be long before it reaches major cities."

Russian General Anatoly Sergeyevsky, his face lined with stress, nodded grimly. "Our intelligence is the same. Every attempt to enter the town has ended in failure. No communication from the soldiers sent in. It's as if they've vanished into thin air."

Across the table, China's envoy, Xu Li, shifted uncomfortably. "This is not a mere natural disaster. There are forces at play here that defy our understanding. This mansion... this 'Nightmare Mansion,' as the locals have called it, is at the center of everything. We've reviewed the intelligence gathered from the task force that went in. Those experts—"

"All dead," Elena finished, her voice heavy with frustration. "Every single one of them. And the last satellite feed we had before the area went dark... it showed something far worse. The mansion is... growing. Expanding."

A murmur spread through the room as the implications set in.

British Prime Minister Nigel Howard cleared his throat, breaking the uneasy silence. "If what we've uncovered is true, then we aren't dealing with something localized. This is a global threat. Our top scientists believe the Blood Moon isn't just a celestial event. Its influence was somehow connected to the mansion. And now that connection has been severed—or rather, transformed—it's allowing the mansion's influence to spread beyond its walls."

"We have to consider more aggressive measures," Xu Li said, her tone cold but practical. "Containment isn't working. We need to think about elimination."

"Elimination?" Ambassador Vargas' eyes narrowed. "What exactly are you proposing?"

"Nuclear," Xu replied bluntly. "We know the mansion is the source. A tactical strike, before it spreads any further."

The room fell into a tense silence. General Sergeyevsky shook his head. "You think a nuclear strike will destroy whatever evil resides there? You risk unleashing something far worse. This isn't just a structure. It's... it's ancient, and it's tied to forces we don't understand."

The French representative, Amélie Marchand, who had been quiet throughout the discussion, finally spoke, her voice measured. "I agree with General Sergeyevsky. We've received classified reports of the Ritual of Despair that bound the mansion to these dark forces. It's not simply the mansion that is the threat—it's the forces within it. A nuclear strike could backfire. It could... amplify whatever is happening."

A cold silence settled over the room as the leaders absorbed the gravity of her words.

"What about containment on a massive scale?" Prime Minister Howard suggested. "We quarantine the entire region, enforce a no-fly zone, and surround the area with military forces to prevent anyone or anything from leaving."

General Sergeyevsky shook his head. "Containment is only delaying the inevitable. The mansion's influence grows stronger with each death, each soul it consumes. We can't hold back something that feeds on despair and fear. It will find a way out."

Elena leaned back in her chair, rubbing her temples. "So what do we do? We can't nuke it, we can't contain it... what's left? Sit back and wait for it to consume us all?"

Just as the room seemed to descend into hopelessness, a tall figure entered, a man dressed in a dark suit, his face solemn and lined with the weight of secrets. Dr. Jonathan Hayes, a leading authority on metaphysical phenomena and occult history, stepped forward, placing a thick folder on the table before the council.

"You don't understand what you're dealing with," Hayes said, his voice low but commanding. "The Nightmare Mansion is not just a haunted house. It's a living entity, a nexus of dark energy tied to ancient rituals that have been forgotten by the modern world. The Ritual of Despair that bound the mansion to these forces has been completed. And now, its influence is spreading—because it no longer needs to stay contained."

Hayes opened the folder, revealing old maps, pages from ancient tomes, and photographs of strange symbols carved into the mansion's stone walls. "This isn't just about Ravenswood or even the surrounding towns. The mansion is connected to ley lines—powerful, natural energy channels that crisscross the globe. With each soul it consumes, its power grows, and now it's beginning to tap into those ley lines. Soon, it won't need to stay in one place. It could manifest anywhere—everywhere."

The room erupted in murmurs, the gravity of the situation finally becoming clear.

"Is there any way to stop it?" Ambassador Vargas asked, her voice shaking slightly.

Hayes looked at her, his eyes dark with knowledge that none of them wanted to hear. "There may be a way... but it would require a new task force, one trained not just in modern warfare, but in the arcane, in rituals and counter-magics that predate even the mansion itself. We'll need experts in mythology, metaphysics, and, quite frankly, those who have dealt with things beyond the veil of reality."

"And if that doesn't work?" General Sergeyevsky asked, his voice gruff.

Hayes' silence was answer enough. Finally, he spoke, his voice grim. "Then we are facing something far worse than we ever imagined. This mansion... this entity... will spread its influence across the world. And once it reaches the ley lines, it could tear through reality itself."

The room fell into a deep, oppressive silence.

"We don't have much time," Hayes said quietly. "The Nightmare Mansion is awake now. And it won't stop until it has devoured everything."

As the leaders prepared for what would come next, the dark fog continued to spread, slowly, silently, creeping toward the heart of civilization. The world was on the brink of an infernal revelation, and even as plans were laid, an ominous sense of dread settled over those who knew that the true nightmare had only just begun.

And in the distance, from the heart of the fog, a new whisper began to emerge—a voice carried on the wind, growing stronger with each passing moment.

The mansion had awakened.

Nightmare Mansion: Infernal Revelations awaited.

Message from the Author:

I hope you enjoyed this book, I love astrology and knew there was not a book such as this out on the shelf. I love metaphysical items as well. Please check out my other books:

-Life of Government Benefits

-My life of Hell

-My life with Hydrocephalus

-Red Sky

-World Domination:Woman's rule

-World Domination:Woman's Rule 2: The War

-Life and Banishment of Apophis: book 1

-The Kidney Friendly Diet

-The Ultimate Hemp Cookbook

-Creating a Dispensary(legally)

-Cleanliness throughout life: the importance of showering from childhood to adulthood.

-Strong Roots: The Risks of Overcoddling children

-Hemp Horoscopes: Cosmic Insights and Earthly Healing

- Celestial Hemp Navigating the Zodiac: Through the Green Cosmos

-Astrological Hemp: Aligning The Stars with Earth's Ancient Herb

-The Astrological Guide to Hemp: Stars, Signs, and Sacred Leaves

-Green Growth: Innovative Marketing Strategies for your Hemp Products and Dispensary

-Cosmic Cannabis

-Astrological Munchies

-Henry The Hemp

-Zodiacal Roots: The Astrological Soul Of Hemp

- **Green Constellations: Intersection of Hemp and Zodiac**

-Hemp in The Houses: An astrological Adventure Through The Cannabis Galaxy

-Galactic Ganja Guide

Heavenly Hemp

Zodiac Leaves

Doctor Who Astrology

Cannastrology

Stellar Satvias and Cosmic Indicas

Celestial Cannabis: A Zodiac Journey

AstroHerbology: The Sky and The Soil: Volume 1

AstroHerbology:Celestial Cannabis:Volume 2

Cosmic Cannabis Cultivation

The Starry Guide to Herbal Harmony: Volume 1

The Starry Guide to Herbal Harmony: Cannabis Universe: Volume

2

Yugioh Astrology: Astrological Guide to Deck, Duels and more

Nightmare Mansion: Echoes of The Abyss

Nightmare Mansion 2: Legacy of Shadows

Nightmare Mansion 3: Shadows of the Forgotten

Nightmare Mansion 4: Echoes of the Damned

The Life and Banishment of Apophis: Book 2

Nightmare Mansion: Halls of Despair

Healing with Herb: Cannabis and Hydrocephalus

Planetary Pot: Aligning with Astrological Herbs: Volume 1

Fast Track to Freedom: 30 Days to Financial Independence Using AI, Assets, and Agile Hustles

Cosmic Hemp Pathways

How to Become Financially Free in 30 Days: 10,000 Paths to Prosperity

Zodiacal Herbage: Astrological Insights: Volume 1

Nightmare Mansion: Whispers in the Walls

The Daleks Invade Atlantis

Henry the hemp and Hydrocephalus

10X The Kidney Friendly Diet

Cannabis Universe: Adult coloring book

Hemp Astrology: The Healing Power of the Stars

Zodiacal Herbage: Astrological Insights: Cannabis Universe: Volume 2

Planetary Pot: Aligning with Astrological Herbs: Cannabis Universes: Volume 2

Doctor Who Meets the Replicators and SG-1: The Ultimate Battle for Survival

Nightmare Mansion: Curse of the Blood Moon

The Celestial Stoner: A Guide to the Zodiac

Cosmic Pleasures: Sex Toy Astrology for Every Sign

Hydrocephalus Astrology: Navigating the Stars and Healing Waters

Lapis and the Mischievous Chocolate Bar

Celestial Positions: Sexual Astrology for Every Sign

Apophis's Shadow Work Journal: : A Journey of Self-Discovery and Healing

Kinky Cosmos: Sexual Kink Astrology for Every Sign

Digital Cosmos: The Astrological Digimon Compendium

Stellar Seeds: The Cosmic Guide to Growing with Astrology

Apophis's Daily Gratitude Journal

Cat Astrology: Feline Mysteries of the Cosmos

The Cosmic Kama Sutra: An Astrological Guide to Sexual Positions

Unleash Your Potential: A Guided Journal Powered by AI Insights

Whispers of the Enchanted Grove

Cosmic Pleasures: An Astrological Guide to Sexual Kinks

369, 12 Manifestation Journal

Whisper of the nocturne journal(blank journal for writing or drawing)

The Boogey Book

Locked In Reflection: A Chastity Journey Through Locktober

Generating Wealth Quickly:

How to Generate $100,000 in 24 Hours

Star Magic: Harness the Power of the Universe

The Flatulence Chronicles: A Fart Journal for Self-Discovery

The Doctor and The Death Moth

Seize the Day: A Personal Seizure Tracking Journal

The Ultimate Boogeyman Safari: A Journey into the Boogie World and Beyond

Whispers of Samhain: 1,000 Spells of Love, Luck, and Lunar Magic: Samhain Spell Book

Apophis's guides:

Witch's Spellbook Crafting Guide for Halloween

<u>Frost & Flame: The Enchanted Yule Grimoire of 1000 Winter Spells</u>

<u>The Ultimate Boogey Goo Guide & Spooky Activities for Halloween Fun</u>

Harmony of the Scales: A Libra's Spellcraft for Balance and Beauty

The Enchanted Advent: 36 Days of Christmas Wonders

If you want solar for your home go here: https://www.harborso-lar.live/apophisenterprises/

Get Some Tarot cards: https://www.makeplayingcards.com/sell/ apophis-occult-shop

Get some shirts: https://www.bonfire.com/store/apophis-shirt-emporium/

Instagrams:
@apophis_enterprises,
@apophisbookemporium,
@apophisscardshop
Twitter: @apophisenterpr1
Tiktok:@apophisenterprise
Youtube: @sg1fan23477, @FiresideRetreatKingdom

Podcast: Apophis Chat Zone: https://open.spotify.com/show/ 5zXbrCLEV2xzCp8ybrfHsk?si=fb4d4fdbdce44dec

Newsletter: https://apophiss-newsletter-27c897.beehiiv.com/

Milton Keynes UK
Ingram Content Group UK Ltd.
UKHW042126211024
450028UK00010B/131